CW00557913

*Hotel Andro*

Gabriel Josipovici was born in Nice in 1940 of Russo-Italian, Romano-Levantine parents. He lived in Egypt from 1945 to 1956, when he came to Britain. After graduating from Oxford he joined the faculty of the University of Sussex in 1963, where he remained till he took early retirement in 1998. He is the author of sixteen novels, three volumes of short stories, eight critical works, a memoir of his mother, the poet and translator Sacha Rabinovitch, and numerous stage and radio plays, and is a regular contributor to the *Times Literary Supplement*. His work has been translated into the major European languages and Arabic. Visit www.gabrieljosipovici.org for further information.

Also by Gabriel Josipovici

Fiction

*The Inventory* (1968)
*Words* (1971)
*Mobius the Stripper: Stories and Short Plays* (1974)
*The Present* (1975)
*Four Stories* (1977)
*Migrations* (1977)
*The Echo Chamber* (1979)
*The Air We Breathe* (1981)
*Conversations in Another Room* (1984)
*Contre Jour: A Triptych after Pierre Bonnard* (1986)
*In the Fertile Land* (1987)
*Steps: Selected Fiction and Drama* (1990)
*The Big Glass* (1991)
*In a Hotel Garden* (1993)
*Moo Pak* (1994)
*Now* (1998)
*Goldberg: Variations* (2002)
*Everything Passes* (2006)
*Two Novels: After* and *Making Mistakes* (2009)
*Heart's Wings* (2010)
*Infinity: The Story of a Moment* (2012)

Theatre

*Vergil Dying* (1977)

Non-fiction

*The World and the Book* (1971, 1979)
*The Lessons of Modernism* (1977, 1987)
*Writing and the Body* (1982)
*The Mirror of Criticism: Selected Reviews* (1983)
*The Book of God: A Response to the Bible* (1988, 1990)
*Text and Voice: Essays 1981–1991* (1992)
*A Life* (2001)
*The Singer on the Shore: Essays 1991–2004* (2006)
*What Ever Happened to Modernism?* (2010)
(ed.) *The Modern English Novel: The Reader, the Writer and the Book* (1975)
(ed.) *The Siren's Song: Selected Essays of Maurice Blanchot* (1980)
(ed. with Brian Cummings) *The Spirit of England: Selected Essays of Stephen Medcalf* (2010)

GABRIEL JOSIPOVICI

# Hotel Andromeda
## A Novel

**CARCANET**

First published in Great Britain in 2014 by
Carcanet Press Limited
Alliance House
Cross Street
Manchester M2 7AQ

www.carcanet.co.uk

A CIP catalogue record for this book is available from the British Library

ISBN 978 1 84777 263 3

The publisher acknowledges financial assistance from Arts Council England

Typeset in Monotype Centaur by XL Publishing Services, Exmouth
Printed and bound in England by SRP Ltd, Exeter

*For Tamar*

*What if these stones*
*Fall into the sea? What if someone builds*
*A stone monument at the sea's edge?*

Yannis Ritsos

## Conversation at the Top of the House

She likes to come up here, to the bright flat at the top of the house, and to sit with the old lady in her large kitchen, with its window open to the sky.

The old lady says:

— I've only got cubes.

She is standing on a chair and rummaging about on the top shelf of the cupboard.

Helena says:

— That's fine. I like cubes.

— Good, the old lady says. Because it's all I've got.

She climbs down, clutching a blue cardboard box.

Helena says:

— I prefer cubes, actually.

— Cubes keep better, the old lady says. The granulated stuff tends to coagulate after a while, so it's silly to get it since you're the only person I know who takes sugar and you don't come to see me that often.

— Don't say that, Helena says.

— It's the truth, isn't it? the old lady says.

— It most certainly isn't, Helena says. I come all the time. In fact I have to stop myself coming up here for fear of becoming a bore.

— There's no danger of that, the old lady says.

— Isn't there?

— None at all. And what's more, you know it.

— I don't, Helena says. But I do know that you're much too polite to say if I bore you.

— That shows how little you know me, the old lady says. If you knew me better you'd know that I always speak my mind.

— You always say that, Helena says, but I doubt if you really do. Not when you think it would hurt someone.

— I value my privacy just as much as anyone else, the old lady says. You don't have to worry. I'll tell you when I don't want to see you. Go on, she says, nodding towards the box, help yourself.

Helena eases a cube out of the box and lets it slide into her cup of tea. They both watch as it slowly disintegrates and merges with the brown liquid.

The old lady says:

— In Russia, before the Revolution, my mother told me, there was one cube of sugar for the whole family. It hung over the table, attached to the lamp cord by a piece of string, and anyone who wanted to sweeten their tea pulled it towards them and had a suck.

— I wouldn't like to have been the youngest, Helena says.

— You wouldn't have minded, the old lady says. Not if you'd not known anything else.

— That's true, Helena says.

— Talking of Russia, the old lady says, have you heard from your sister?

— No, Helena says. You know she never writes.

The old lady takes a cigarette from the packet on the table

in front of her and puts it in her mouth. She lights it and inhales deeply, then lets the smoke trickle out through her nostrils. She puts the lighter down beside the open packet.

Helena says:

— You know very well she doesn't.

— She could email you, the old lady says.

— Email? Helena says. You must be joking, Ruth.

— Why? the old lady says. She must use email for her work.

— I doubt it, Helena says. I doubt if anyone has email there except the government. They barely have telephones.

She stirs her tea and takes a sip.

— And you don't write? the old lady asks.

— Not any more, Helena says.

— You don't want to know what she's up to?

— Of course I do, Helena says. But I told you. What's the point? She never answers my letters. Perhaps she never gets them. I don't know. But I can't keep writing into the silence.

The old lady presses the stub of her cigarette into the ashtray.

Helena says:

— When I was coming up the stairs just now I had the impression someone was looking at me.

She looks down at her cup. She says:

— I sometimes dream that I'm writing to her. And when I'm waking up or sitting in the bus I often find I'm composing a letter to her in my head. Telling her about my work. Trying to explain. But even in my dreams she never replies.

The old lady helps herself to another cup of tea. — For you? she asks.

Helena shakes her head. She says:

— As far as she's concerned I don't exist.

— That's what you think, the old lady says.

— Yes, Helena says. That's what I think.

— But you could be wrong, the old lady says.

— I could. But I know her well enough to think I'm right.

— Well, the old lady says. It's possible.

Helena says:

— As far as she's concerned I'm just a boring old art historian in boring old London.

She stirs the sugar at the bottom of her cup.

— You're not boring, the old lady says. And I've personally never found London boring.

— To her I am and it is, Helena says.

— Perhaps to her, the old lady says. But not to me.

— You're sweet, Helena says.

— I'm not sweet, the old lady says. It's just a fact. Anyway, you're you. Not this and not that. Just you. Nobody else.

— That's what I keep telling myself, Helena says. But at times it's difficult to believe.

— For you what you do is important, the old lady says. That's all that matters.

— Is it? Helena says.

— Of course, the old lady says.

— I'm not so sure, Helena says. If it's of no importance to anyone else then surely I'm kidding myself when I think it's important?

— Why kidding? the old lady says. You may be right and everyone else wrong and one of these days they'll wake up to the fact.

— And if everyone else is right?

– It's still important if it's important to you.

– That's hard to hold on to, Helena says.

– Of course, the old lady says, in the great scheme of things it's not important. But then nothing is.

– So?

– But there's something between the great scheme of things and pure self-indulgence, isn't there? the old lady asks.

Helena says:

– I know what you mean, but it's hard to keep believing. I mean I believe when I'm at my desk working. I really do. I know it's important to get it right and if it's important to get it right then that means there's a right and a wrong and it's outside myself. Call it truth. Or something. But the rest of the time, away from my desk...

– That's true of everyone, the old lady says.

– Not of Alice, Helena says. She's never doubted for an instant that what she's doing is important. And she's right. It is.

– That's what you think, the old lady says. Perhaps she thinks the same of you.

– Oh no, Helena says. She's always known exactly what she wanted to do. And then she's gone and done it.

– If that's true, the old lady says, then she's very lucky.

– But why are some people lucky? Helena says, pouring herself another cup of tea.

– If we knew that we wouldn't call it luck, would we? the old lady says. On the other hand perhaps we imagine they never had any doubts because that suits us. Like George, my nephew. He seemed to know from the start that he wanted to be a concert pianist and that's what he became. He lives for his piano and he lives for his performances. He doesn't have a family and he doesn't have any hobbies. When he isn't practising he's reading detective stories. It relaxes him, he says, after hours at the piano. And the hours more he's going to put in before he goes to bed. But I sometimes wonder whether he doesn't ask himself why he's done what he's done, since he's never reached the pinnacle of his profession.

— He's done pretty well, Helena says. He's always on the radio.

— Pretty well, the old lady says. But he's never reached the top. Where you find the Barenboims and the Schiffs. What I mean is that if he hadn't existed it would not have made much difference to music. So perhaps he wonders whether it was worth all the sacrifices just to get to the second rank.

— There aren't any ranks in Alice's line of work, Helena says.

— That's true, the old lady says.

Helena swallows down the last of her tea and pushes the cup away from her as the curtains suddenly billow in the breeze.

The old lady gets up to shut the window.

— Gerald keeps urging me to find a ground floor flat, she says. I tell him climbing the stairs is what keeps me fit. And I wouldn't give this up for anything.

— I can't imagine you anywhere else, Helena says.

— I'm on top of the world, the old lady says. Let me enjoy it while I can.

## And in the Basement

She holds the postcard photo out to him. — What would you say he was thinking? she asks.

He examines it in silence.

He looks up at her. He says:

— Nothing.

— Nothing?

— He's just feeling the sun on his face, he says.

— But what's going through his mind?

— Nothing, he says. I just told you: Nothing.

— All right, she says. What's he feeling in the pit of his stomach then?

He leans over the photo again.

A time.

He hands it to her across the table. He says:

— I don't know.

She says:

— It's the end of his life. He's seventy-one, seventy-two. He's lost the two people who were central to his life, his crippled brother and his philistine and domineering mother. He's an old man sitting in his back garden. His yard, as he would have said. Sitting not on a bench but on a kitchen chair. The chair that was always there in the yard. Under the quince tree.

She looks at him. He shrugs.

— Well? she says.

— I told you.

— Nothing?

— Uhuh.

— Nobody's that empty, she says.

— Who said empty?

— You did.

— I said nothing was going through his mind. That's different.

She waits.

He looks down at the table.

— Go on, she says.

— He's just an old man sitting on a chair under a quince tree in his yard in the sun, he says.

— And?

— What more do you want?

— I don't know, she says.

— Can't you be satisfied with that?

— Is he happy, do you think?

— It's not a question I'd ask, he says.

— But I'm asking it. Is he happy?

— Wittgenstein was a pretty tormented man, he says. The very English Bertrand Russell couldn't make out this angst-ridden Austrian Jew. But as he was dying Wittgenstein is supposed to have said: 'Please tell them I've had a wonderful life.'

— What's that supposed to mean? she says.

— It means that most of us can't ever really decide whether we're happy or unhappy. Sometimes we think the one thing and sometimes the other. And there's no-one to turn to for arbitration.

She leans over and lays another card-photo on the table in front of him.

— What's this? he says, drawing it towards him.

— Look, she says.

— I'm looking, he says.

— Tell me what you see.

— It's him again. In a room. Same photographer no doubt. He turns the card over. — Hans Namuth, he says.

— Go on, she says.

He examines the photo again.

A time.

He says:

— Same period, probably the same shoot. He sits in a broken-down armchair in front of a window with a frilly curtain half drawn back and the most amazing wallpaper, like the interior of a woodland glen that hasn't seen the light of the sun for years. He's looking down, his eyes closed, his left hand on his knee and his right clenched round a book which he seems to be pressing into his huge bony forehead. Or perhaps he's just meant to be leaning his head against it. It's difficult to tell. Next to the window enclave is a narrow door with a No Smoking sign stuck on it, and, below that, a number of other pieces of paper, some of them whole sheets. A wall which starts barely beyond the door juts out towards us, holding him and us in the tiny space, made smaller by the fact that it's entirely taken up with shelves bulging with files and loose sheets of paper, in front of which stand boxes also filled with papers and files, on one of which one can make out the words: 'Records and Music'. But the predominant atmosphere is of a demented silence.

She says:

— Yes. The silence is pretty deafening.

— Can you make out the title of the book he's holding? he asks.

— No, she says. I even tried with a magnifying glass, but it's blurred.

He goes on looking at the photo.

She says:

— His brother's died. His mother's died. He's all alone. But then he was always alone. His mother wanted him to be what he wasn't and would never be, a social and financial success, someone who would help her keep up the 'tone' she was used to from her own upbringing, someone she could boast about to her friends. She couldn't make him out. Why was he so lacking in ambition? Why couldn't he earn a proper living? Why did he have to take those dead-end jobs, like working in a garden centre right there in Queens? Why did he have to spend so much time with those screwball Christian Scientists and poring over the works of Mary Baker Eddy? And yet, despite all this, famous artists like Willem de Kooning and Marcel Duchamp would ring up and ask how he was, and famous ballerinas like Tamara Toumanova and Zizi Jeanmaire, and film stars like Tony Curtis, would come round to the house to see him and buy his work. Tony Curtis called the other day, she would tell her friends. Tony Curtis? *The* Tony Curtis? Of course. Who else? He's a great admirer of Joe's work. His younger brother had had cerebral palsy since early childhood. He was never able to walk and spent his life in a wheelchair. He had difficulty speaking but was not in any way mentally retarded. He and Joseph were very close. Almost like identical twins. Each knew what the other was feeling, even when they were apart. Coming home from work Joseph would spend hours playing toy trains with Robert, two men in their thirties and forties playing toy trains. The three of them, the mother and two brothers, lived together all their lives, after their two sisters got married and moved out, and it drove Joseph mad. He worked at night on the kitchen table. If his mother found one of his boxes on the table when she came down in the morning she would throw it out into the yard. Kent you keep your stuff out of my kitchen? Looket the mess you've made! But he went on making those boxes. For himself. To give to the starlets he worshipped. To the shop assistants he hardly dared talk to. To the artists he venerated. Duchamp owned one. Man Ray another. My son who knows Willem de Kooning. Moira Shearer. Susan Sontag. And she kept throwing them into the yard. If he had forgotten one in the oven, where he would often put them to create the cracked and ageing quality he was after, she would scream at him until he put his hands over his ears. 'She screamed at and scolded this fifty-year-old man as if he was seven years old,' one visitor commented. 'It was unbelievable.'

She stops.

He waits.

He gets up and goes to the bookshelf. He pulls down a book and brings it back to the table. He sits down, flicks through the book till he finds what he wants, then pushes it across the table to her.

She asks:

— What's this?

He says:

— Read.

— 'Old Man Asleep?' she asks.

— Uhuh.

She reads. He sits opposite her and watches her.

— Yes, she says, when she has done, pushing the book back across the table to him.

He turns it round and reads for himself.

He says: — Sorry. The title fooled me.

She waits.

He turns the pages. — Ah, he says, here's what I was looking for.

He pushes the book across the table to her again. He says:

— Read it aloud.

— Title and all?

He laughs. — Forget the title, he says.

She reads: —

Weaker and weaker, the sunlight falls
In the afternoon. The proud and the strong
Have departed.

Those that are left are the unaccomplished,
The finally human,
Natives of a dwindled sphere.

Their indigence is an indigence
That is an indigence of the light,
A stellar pallor that hangs on the threads.

Little by little, the poverty
Of autumnal space becomes
A look, a few words spoken.

Each person completely touches us
With what he is and as he is,
In the stale grandeur of annihilation.

— Yes, she says. I like that. The unaccomplished, the finally human.

He repeats:

— Their indigence is an indigence that is an indigence of the light, a stellar pallor that hangs on the threads.

They are silent, listening again to the poem.

— Indigence? she asks.

— Poverty, he says. Need.

— That's rather what it sounded like, she says. And the title?

— One of Stevens' jokes, he says.

— I'm not sure I can work it out.

— *Lebensweisheit*, he says, means knowledge of life, wisdom. *Spielerei* means playing.

— And the whole thing?

— Work it out.

— Playing at wisdom?

— Something like that.

— Pompous German philosophers?

— That too.

She reads the poem to herself.

She says:

— I like it.

— It's your man, he says. One of the unaccomplished, the finally human. Native of a dwindled sphere. That's what he looks like to me, at any rate, sitting there on his chair under the quince tree with the sun on his face.

— And in the room?

— Even more in the room.

She ponders.

She says:

— Maybe you're right. Maybe that's all that can be said of him. And yet there's something missing. It's too fine. A modern icon. Or perhaps it's just that it works in poetry but not in the messy prose of life. The prose that has to take into account the seconds ticking by on the face of the watch, the physical ailments of age, the tug of memories and of all the failed dreams and ambitions. This is an old man who's lost everything. Who's just waiting for the end. I sense a terror there. Although I grant you there's something else. Perhaps a kind of grandeur. I don't know.

He says:

— I'm talking about the photos you've just shown me. You're bringing all you know about him and his life to bear on them and I'm not sure it's helping you.

— Maybe, she says. But it's the photos that haunt me. If only I knew how to deal with them. But I don't. And they won't let me go. I sometimes think I embarked on the book simply to understand what they mean to me, and yet at every stage I fall back from it in impotent rage, feeling they are an indictment of what I'm doing. I can't do anything with them and I can't let them go.

— That only means you haven't finished the book, he says.

— You think so?

— Sure, he says.

— Why sure?

He shrugs.

— You really think so?

— Come here, he says.

— What?

— Come here.

— What for?

— Come and sit on my lap.

— What for?

— Oh for Christ's sake, Helena, he says. You don't want me to spell it out?

— I don't have time, she says. I have my book to write.

— Just for a moment.

— Don't be a bore, Tom, she says.

He shrugs his shoulders. — Never mind, he says. Another time.

She gets up.

— Thanks for the coffee, she says.

— My pleasure, he says.

He listens to her footsteps on the basement stairs outside the window and then on the steps of the house; he hears her insert her key into the lock of the front door, her footsteps in the hall, her insertion of the key into her own door, and finally her footsteps, muffled by the carpet, over his head.

## An Unexpected Phone Call

The phone rings. She picks it up.

— Helena?

A male voice. She does not recognise it.

It repeats:

— Helena?

— Who is it? she asks.

— Is this Helena?

— Yes. Who is it please?

— Ah, he says. I am a friend of Alice. She give me your number.

— Alice?

— I am a friend.

— A friend of Alice's?

— She give me your number.

— When? she says. Where?

— She said you can put me up.

— Me?

— She said.

— Alice said I could put you up?

— Yes.

— I see.

There is a silence at the other end.

Finally she says: — For how long?

— She said.

— Yes but for how long?

— How long?

She waits.

— Two-three days, he says at last.

She asks:

— You're from there?

— Pardon me?

— You've come from Grozny?

— I just arrive.

— I see.

He waits.

Finally he says: — Please you can put me up?

— You haven't anywhere to stay?

— She said.

— Not to me.

— Pardon me?

— She didn't say anything to me.

He is silent.

She asks:

— She gave you my number?

— Yes, he says.

The phone goes dead. She puts down the receiver, waits.
It rings again.

She picks it up. She says:

— Yes?

He asks:

— You can put me up?

She waits.

— She said, the man says again.

— Where are you?

— The aeroport.

— Heathrow?

— Yes.

— You've just arrived?

— Yes.

— And Alice told you I could put you up?

— Yes.

— I see.

He waits.

— It's not very convenient, she says. I work at home. There isn't much room here.

He waits.

She asks:

— You don't have anywhere else to stay?

— No.

— All right, she says. Do you know how to get here?

— Give me address, he says. I will tell taxi.

— You have a pen?

— Give me, he says.

When she has done so he says:

— All right. I will tell taxi.

— You might be better off taking the tube, she says.

— Pardon me?

— It might be easier to take the underground at this time of day.

— No problem, he says.

— It's flat two, she says. Ring and I'll let you in.

— No problem, he says.

## The Arrival of the Man from Grozny

The buzzer sounds.

She goes out into the entrance and opens the front door.

— Helena?

She stands, looking at him.

— Please, he says. You have money for taxi?

— I thought you were taking the tube?

— Please. He is waiting.

— You don't have money?

— No English money.

— Why didn't you change at the airport?

He stands there, his shoulder bag slung round his neck.

— How much? she says.

— Twenty-six pounds.

— Why didn't you take the underground?

— I don't have money.

— Why didn't you change at Heathrow?

— I give you back, he says, standing there.

— Wait, she says.

When she returns he hasn't moved. She thrusts the money into his hand. She says:

— Make sure he gives you back the change.

He runs down the steps, his shoulder bag flapping.

She waits.

When he returns he is carrying a smart new suitcase with
wheels.

— You brought the change? she says.

He hands it to her.

— Come inside, she says. The front door shuts by itself.

She stands aside to let him enter the flat, closes the door.

— I'll show you where you're sleeping, she says.

She leads the way down the corridor.

— There's not much room, she says. Perhaps Alice
explained.

— No problem, he says.

— Perhaps you thought I lived in a palace? With hordes of
servants?

She holds the door open and stands aside for him to enter.

— Pardon me? he says.

He edges past her into the tiny room.

— She could have asked me first.

He is silent.

— It doesn't surprise me, though, she says.

He puts his shoulder bag down on the bed.

— I have a message, he says.

— From Alice?

— Yes.

— A letter?

— No.

— It was too much to hope for, she says.

— Pardon me?

They stand side by side in the narrow room.

— The message, she says. What is it?

— She says to tell you she thinks of you the whole time.

— The whole time?

— Yes.

— Remarkable, she says.

— Pardon me? he says.

She sits down on the bed. He stands next to her, the shiny new suitcase beside him.

— That's funny, she says.

— Funny?

— You know my sister?

— Pardon me?

— You know Alice?

— Of course.

— Do you think she thinks about me the whole time?

He stands. He looks very tired.

— Well? she says, looking up at him. Do you?

— Pardon me?

— As someone who knows her, would you say she was thinking about me the whole time? Would you?

— I don't know, he says.

— But that was the message?

— Yes.

— What would you guess?

He stands, one hand on the shoulder-bag.

— When you go back, she says. You are going back?

— Maybe, he says.

— Well, if you do, when you do, will you give her a message from me?

— No problem, he says.

— Will you tell her I think about her the whole time too?

He stands, swaying slightly.

– You won't forget?

– No problem, he says.

– But you're not sure you're going back?

– No.

– Well, she says, if you do, remember to tell her that I think about her the whole time too.

He waits, swaying slightly in the narrow room.

– I'll get you some towels, she says, standing up.

When she returns he hasn't moved. She puts the towels down on the bed. – The bathroom's next door, she says. Sleep as long as you like. I won't wake you.

– Thank you, he says.

She goes out, closing the door behind her.

## A Walk Along the Towpath

Under some of the road bridges that line the towpath you have to walk in single file. Under one or two you even have to stoop.

— I was here in 1988, he says, as they resume their walk side by side.

— You were working?

— No. Student.

— What were you studying?

— Only language student, he says.

— You were doing a language course?

— Yes.

— Where did you stay?

— Cromwell Road. A big house. But the rooms were very small. So small. The ceilings were very high but the rooms were very small. Like that you know they have been cut from bigger rooms.

She glances at her watch.

— In my profession, he says, you become used to live rough. But what I do not like is…how you say?… I do not like when everything shouts at you that people are trying to make so much money as they can from you.

— Greed, she says.

— Yes, he says. Greed.

— We should go back, she says. I have work to do.

— You write books about artists?

— Yes. Sort of.

— Alice says.

— Alice despises what I do, she says.

— Pardon me?

— She spits at what I do.

— No no, he protests. She always speak of you with respect.

— Really?

— Of course.

— She's never read any of my books.

— Of course, he says again.

— What do you mean of course? she says.

— She show me.

— She showed you my books?

— Of course.

— You amaze me, she says. I send them to her but I always thought she threw them away as soon as she got them, if she ever got them.

— She show me, he says. She say you are much respected in England.

— She's never taken the trouble to acknowledge any of them, she says. Let alone read them and tell me what she thinks.

They walk shoulder to shoulder along the narrow towpath.

— How many read your books? he asks.

She laughs.

— Why you laugh? he asks.

— You want to know?

— Of course.

– Twenty-five, she says.

– Twenty-five thousand?

– No, she says. Twenty-five.

– I do not believe, he says.

– Honest.

– I do not believe.

– Perhaps a bit more, she says. Let's say fifty.

They reach another bridge and he lets her go first. When they are side by side he says again:

– Why you write such books?

She laughs.

– Why?

– It's a good question, she says. Probably because they are the only books I know how to write. Or perhaps they're the only books I want to write. Or perhaps that's the same thing.

– And how you live? he asks.

– Oh that, she says. That's another story.

They walk.

– Our parents left us both enough to get by. You could say I was cursed with a small private income.

They walk.

– How many books you have written? he asks.

– A fair number.

– Pardon me?

– Quite a few.

– How many?

– Less than twenty-five, she says, laughing.

– Which one you like best?

She laughs again.

– Why you laugh? he asks.

— I don't know, she says. I never asked myself that question.

He walks at her shoulder.

— Perhaps a book about a French painter called Bonnard, she says.

— Ah, Bonnard, he says.

— You've heard of him?

— Who has not heard?

They walk.

— I like his modesty, she says. His quietness. Though his art is hardly modest. It's quite ambitious really. But mysterious.

— Why?

— You'll have to read my book to find out, she says.

— You have at home?

— I expect so, yes.

— Then I will read.

— I doubt if you'll have the time, she says.

— I have time, he says.

They walk.

— I thought you were only here for a day or two, she says.

— Yes, he says. I have to see some people.

— About work?

— Yes.

— Papers?

— Papers. Agencies. Who will give me work.

— You're going back to Chechnya?

— That is not possible at the moment.

— Why?

— It is not possible.

— They threw you out?

– It is not possible.

– What did you do that they didn't like?

– With all these regimes you cannot say. They give you your papers. They put the stamping on it all correct. And then suddenly: Out.

– You did something you shouldn't have?

– I speak to people.

– People you shouldn't have spoken to?

– People. You know?

They walk.

– And I take photos.

– They didn't like that?

– No.

– But I thought that was your job? I thought you were there as a photographer?

– Yes.

– But they only wanted photographs of the things they wanted photographed? Is that it?

– Yes.

They walk.

– I want you to tell me what it's like, she says. I want you to tell me exactly what Alice is doing. How she lives. What her day consists of. All that. But not now. Right?

– Pardon me?

– I'm going to go up to the road here, she says. If you want to go on you'll find your own way back. I've given you the *A to Z*.

– I go back also, he says.

– I don't want to talk, she says. I want to think about my book.

— I also have to think, he says.

— Actually, she says, I'd rather you didn't walk back with me. All right?

— No problem, he says.

— You've got the keys I gave you?

— Yes.

— I'll see you later then, she says.

— No problem, he says.

## *Nom de Plume* or *Nom de Guerre?*

— Make me a coffee, she says, throwing herself into a chair.

— Give me a kiss, he says.

— Please, Tom, she says. Just make me a coffee.

— Not till you give me a kiss.

— Don't be tiresome, she says.

He busies himself with the coffee.

— You've seen my new houseguest? she asks.

— You have a new houseguest?

— I thought you'd have noticed.

— Who is it?

— A Czech journalist from Grozny.

— Grozny? A friend of Alice's?

— That's what he says.

He puts the pot of coffee down on the table in front of her and sits down opposite.

— You don't believe him? he asks.

— Why shouldn't I believe him?

— I thought that's what you were suggesting.

She pours out her coffee.

— Is that why he's here? he asks.

— It's why he's staying with me, yes.

— Her lover?

— I didn't ask. I doubt it.

— Why?

— I don't know. I don't think Alice has time for lovers.

— There's always time for lovers.

— Or the energy.

— Having a lover gives you energy, he says. That's what you never seem to understand.

She puts sugar into her coffee and stirs.

— Anyway, he says, I thought Alice was exceedingly energetic.

— That's what I mean, Helena says. It all goes into her work. She sips her coffee.

— You should ask him, he says.

— Why?

— It's good to know where you stand.

— I know where I stand.

He retrieves a mug from the sink and pours himself some coffee. — Nice chap? he asks.

— OK.

— Why's he here?

— They threw him out.

— But why not Prague if he's Czech?

— He's looking for work.

— He writes in English?

— He's a photographer.

— Ah. And what did he have to say about Alice?

— He says the conditions are intolerable. There's the semblance of order but basically it's a banana republic, Caucasus style: tinpot dictator taking his orders from Moscow, everyone who isn't part of his entourage too frightened to raise their heads, corruption everywhere, the villagers still in shock after two bloody wars, a few partisans determined to fight on, now reinforced by jihadists from over the border. For most people, including Alice and the orphanage, no money, constant abuses from the authorities, feral children who think nothing of stealing whatever is around, abusing the weaker ones, sometimes maiming and even killing them. Otherwise everything's fine.

— Sounds fun, he says.

— Uhuh.

— Alice must like it, if she stays on.

— She wants to help.

She sips her coffee.

— Come and sit on my lap, he says.

— Don't be a bore, she says.

— I just thought we could talk more easily like that.

— I've got to get back to work. I just came down for a cup of coffee.

— Why?

— I'd run out.

— Not to see me?

— Sorry.

He pours himself the last of the coffee. He asks:

— Shall I make some more?

— Not for me, she says.

He drinks.

— How long's he staying? he asks.

— I don't know, she says.

— It's open-ended?

— It's OK, she says. There's the spare bedroom. He's out all day doing the rounds of the papers and the agencies.

— He's hoping to go back?

— I don't think he can. He's looking for another assignment.

— There isn't exactly a shortage of horror places in the world, is there? he says. Where they can send photographers and reporters.

— No.

— But he hasn't found anything yet.

— Not yet, no.

— Alice told you he was coming?

— You know she never communicates.

— She may not even know this guy is staying with you.

— She gave him my phone number.

— True, but who knows when? They may have quarrelled since.

— Everything's possible.

— He could be planning to cut your throat.

— Why would he want to do that?

— I don't know. Sadism. The need for ready cash. There could be all sorts of reasons.

— True.

— Would you like that?

— To have my throat cut?

— To have him cut your throat.

— No.

— Why?

— It might hurt. And I want to live.

— To finish your book?

— Maybe. To finish my book.

— Not because you love me?

– No.

– Bring him down some time, Tom says. Introduce him.

– Uhuh.

– You don't sound very keen.

– No, I don't mind. I will if you like.

– How's it going, by the way?

– What?

– The book.

– So-so.

– Meaning?

– Meaning so-so.

– I see.

He drinks up the last of his coffee. – Mine's taken a different turn, he says.

– A different turn?

– I've started something new.

– You finished the other?

– No. I decided to let it go and start this new thing.

– I have to go, she says.

– You don't want to hear about it?

– Another time, she says.

– It's about two sisters, he says.

– Really?

– Yes, he says. Two sisters. I can tell you more if you like.

– Another time, she says, getting up and making for the door.

– What's his name, by the way? he asks.

– Ed, she says.

– Ed?

– Uhuh.

— It doesn't sound very Czech to me.

— Call me Ed, he said.

— He did? Just like that?

— Just like that.

— Perhaps it's his *nom de plume*, he says.

— Perhaps.

— Or it could be his *nom de guerre*.

— You'll have to ask him.

— I intend to. What kind of photographs has he been taking?

— I've got to go.

— Give me a kiss.

— Tom, she says. Please. I won't be able to drop in for coffee any more if you go on like that.

— OK, he says. Just trying.

— Beware, she says, what you wish for in your youth you may acquire in middle age.

— Is that a threat? he asks.

— No, she says. Just a quotation.

## Hotel Andromeda

She writes, sitting at her desk by the window.

*I have to accept the fact that I am far from liking everything he does. In fact, much of it repels me. The sweetness of it. The tweeness of it. All those Romantic ballerinas and lost girls in woods. All those dolls and that fake snow and real twigs. I don't just not like it very much, I actually dislike it intensely. While other things of his move me deeply. The pale princes in their slot-machine prison-altars. The empty grids against the white backgrounds. The cockatoos. But most of all the series of boxes he made in the fifties concerned with hotels and the stars, and the most moving of those is the mini-series known as* Hotel Andromeda.

She gets up and goes to the kitchen. She lets the cold tap run and fills a glass with water. She drains it, rinses it, turns off the tap.

She returns to her room and sits down at the desk. She bends over the notebook and begins to write again.

She writes:

*I don't know what it is about them that lifts them above the rest. Perhaps it's the fact that while the others often feel merely nostalgic for a world of lost beauty and innocence, which reminds me too much of the kind of Romantic art I most dislike, in these hotel boxes the yoking of hotels and the heavens creates something as true to our time and as resonant as* The Waste Land *and Duchamp's* Large Glass. *It reminds me of Eliot's*

She pushes back the chair and gets up. She goes to the

bookshelf, takes down a book, returns to the desk. She opens it and searches for a while, finds what she wants, picks up her pen.

She writes:

'The boarhound and the boar / Pursue their pattern as before, / But reconciled among the stars.'

She closes the book, pushes it aside.

She writes:

That's in Four Quartets, as it happens, not The Waste Land, but it catches what JC does in these boxes beautifully. Except that perhaps we should not speak of 'reconciled' in connection with them. For what he does is take some Renaissance images and diagrams of the constellations, cut out from the beautiful colour reproductions he found in nineteenth-century popular astronomy books, particularly those of Camille Flammarion, and collage them onto notepaper which once belonged to old, usually French provincial hotels with absurdly grand names, such as Hôtel des Cieux and Grand Hôtel de l'Univers, which he must also have picked up in his wanderings round the junk shops of Manhattan. But these are not simple collages, they are boxes, and by now he is a master of box construction and of the organisation of space which working with boxes entails. In one, for example, the name, Hôtel de l'Etoile, appears at the top of a white page which is partly obscured on the left by a white pillar which runs from top to bottom of the box. In the centre he has placed a black rectangle dotted with what we take to be stars, and at the bottom right some signs of the zodiac, of which the most visible is the ram and a kneeling woman holding a bow in her right hand. The Hotel Andromeda series is more mysterious. In Greek mythology Andromeda, the daughter of Cassiopeia, was chained to a rock as a prey to a sea-monster by Proteus, the God of the Seas, after her mother boasted that she was more beautiful than the Nereids, the sea-nymphs, and was eventually rescued by Perseus. After her death she was turned into *a constellation of the Northern Hemisphere, next to Perseus and her mother. Artists have found the story irresistible, and there are famous paintings of her chained to her rock by Rembrandt, Delacroix and many others. In JC's finest box on the theme the name of the hotel, though partially obscured, seems to be* Grand Hôtel de l'Observatoire, *but above that, in caps, we find the word* ANDROMEDA, *while towards the bottom and half hidden by the white pillar which runs parallel to the frame from top to bottom one can make out the fading fragments* AND EL DE L'UNIV, *as though, spectrally, it was simultaneously the Grand Hôtel de l'Univers. In reality, in Besançon or Le Havre or wherever, it was no doubt just another seedy, run-down establishment, with one bathroom per floor, for the use of which you had to pay a supplement, and a wardrobe taking up half the room, with a door that keeps swinging open even when you are sure you have locked it. For Cornell, however, the name is magical. It carries an aura which over-rides or at least challenges the ocular evidence of the notepaper on which it was printed. In this box Andromeda, in the pose of a trapeze artist of ambiguous gender, with bare upper body turned away from us, right arm stretched out into a square of blazing white, face turned to the right in pure profile and rich head of hair, left arm bent at the elbow, a loose skirt girding the lower body, and strong legs clearly visible, rests on a high wire, in shadow except for that outstretched right arm. Stars cover her body and are visible on the tips of the fingers of her right hand, and a metal chain hangs down from a crossbar that runs parallel to the top of the box, on the left side of which a mysterious griffin head is painted on a lantern or drum, perhaps a cipher for the sea monster. The chain is obviously an allusion to that which once bound Andromeda to her rock, but she is free of it, like Houdini, the escape artist JC saw perform in his youth and never forgot. But the chain also serves to divide the box vertically, as the high wire on which Andromeda sits divides it horizontally. The white pillar on the left reinforces the sense of peering into a distant space, through a window perhaps. Using what appears to be enamel paint on masonite JC creates a mottled effect above and below the figure, suggesting the filmy appearance of a nebula.*

*JC stencilled the figure of Andromeda from a star chart published by Hévélius in 1690, which he found in Camille Flammarion's* Les Etoiles. *One of Hévélius's grid-lines becomes the high-wire on which Andromeda perches, like the stars that seemed to JC to perch like sparrows on the telephone wire across his back yard. The whole image exudes a powerful sense of both human and cosmic balance.*

*Are we in heaven, then, among the myths of antiquity, or in the workshop of a Renaissance magus, or in a seedy French provincial hotel? The box is profoundly ambiguous. On the one hand this is the hotel of all hotels, a place in the heavens open to the stars, inside which (but what is inside and what outside in this heavenly hotel?) Andromeda, free and transformed, performs her glorious trapeze acts for ever and ever. But the fact that the name appears in French on all too ordinary notepaper allows a hint of sadness and even despair to seep into this image of life in the heavens, sadness at the hubris of such a name, despair at the thought of the bleak reality of such places which, far from redeeming time, convey only the sense that time has passed them by.*

Biting her lower lip till it hurts, she presses on.

She writes:

*Both* Hotel Andromeda *and* Hôtel de l'Etoile *mingle the sordid and the heavenly, reality and the ideal, in a way only Cornell, to my knowledge, has ever been able to do. It seems to me much more powerful than Hopper, and goodness knows I like Hopper, for Hopper's world is desperately melancholic and nothing else, though people talk of the poetry of his melancholy and of course there is always a certain poetry in melancholy — but it is not Cornell's way. He is much stranger than that. Much more unsettling. In these boxes there is a constant two-way movement between the mundane and the mythical which reminds me of Proust's wonderful descrip-*

tion of telephone operators as the mediating angels of our age. But Proust's image is basically optimistic, transforming the banalities of modern communication into myth, whereas in Cornell it is impossible to say which triumphs, the seediness evoked by the notepaper or the wonder evoked by the name Andromeda and by the beautiful bisexual body of the trapeze artist, who is at once a desirable athlete, an ancient princess and a constellation visible in the heavens. It is the ambiguity of the box that so draws me, and that ambiguity is never resolved but forces us to move, as in a Möbius strip, perpetually from the one to the other.

She stops. She looks up and gazes into space.

She bends her head again. She writes:

And though Andromeda here in heaven seems to have escaped her chains for ever, transforming them into the accessories of her high-flying trapeze act, we wonder if Cornell, chained to his sick brother and domineering mother, was not creating an image he could long for but never realise. But the glory of the series (for there are several versions) lies in the fact that the box is a dramatisation not of the dream but of both the dream and its source in a life from which there is no escape. Here we are confronted with a glimpse of heaven and the promise of a life at once airborne and meaningful, a world peopled by the heroes and heroines of antiquity, but also a world of dreary French provincial hotels with absurdly grandiose names, hotels in which the tired desk-clerk gives you the key without once looking into your face, in which there are no lifts and the lavatory at the end of the corridor stinks and the windows will not open. Is he lifting our sordid and unhappy world into heaven and myth or dragging myth down to our sordid and unhappy world? The thrill of these boxes is that they provide no answer to this question (I am repeating myself).

These, she writes, are the hotels of our dreams and of our nightmares, the hotels of the lost and the abandoned, where one waits for nothing and where in the next room sex or death is taking its course without any attempt at silence or concealment; but hotels too where inner and outer, self and universe, change places with joyful ease and time itself is abolished.

*I grew up thinking about art as 'the beautiful',* she writes, *but I have come to understand that that is not what art is at all. Art is what manages to express that which lies buried so deep inside us that we can never find the sounds or images or words for it and so could never have access to were it not for others, artists. That is why they mean so much to us. That is why Cornell means so much to me.*

## Thanks to the Russians

— Even if you could see it you could not believe it, he says. Even if you are looking at it in front of you, you cannot believe it.

— I saw the photos in the papers, she says. Everyone saw those.

— Like London in the Blitz. Or Berlin in forty-five, he says. Everyone knows those photos.

He says:

— When I went first you could not believe that people were still living there. Thousands of people. Like rats. In basements filled with rubble. Under the open sky in the corners of buildings with three walls only. I have difficulty to talk about it. Today they try to hide it. Marble presidential palace. Big avenue. Smart uniforms for the police. But that is only façade. In other places it is still like when I first saw it. A whole city in ruin. They would bring the tanks and stand them in what was before the main square of Grozny and fire mortars at the walls that were still standing. Then they would watch as the walls collapsed and the frightened squatters fled. Then they would turn the tanks and roll back to the barracks.

He takes a cigarette out of the packet in front of him, taps it on the back of his hand and puts it in his mouth.

— No, she says.

— I'm sorry.

— I told you, she says. If you want to smoke go outside.

He lays the cigarette down next to the packet on the table in front of him.

— But life went on, he says. It always amazes me, but always life goes on. Schools carried on even if there were no roofs to the classrooms. You won't believe, but once I even saw a jogger in Grozny, running and checking on his watch like they always do. And in the first year there was an old man walking round with a table on his head, the legs sticking up into the air. It's my roof, he would say. It's all I have left and it's the roof over my head. He would stand there in his rags in the middle of the street, balancing the table on his head with one hand and masturbating with the other. With a roof over my head, he said, I can still make love to my wife, no? Her body is under the rubble but no-one can take her out of my head. I had a talk with him once, when he was more calm, sitting on his upturned table by the side of the road. Did you make love to your wife when you lived in your house? I asked him. Not for twenty years, he said, but now, thanks to the Russians, she is young and beautiful as when I first knew her, and I can make love to her again. Whenever I want. How can I thank the Russians enough?

He moves the cigarette to the other side of the box.

He says:

— Alice did not tell you how it was?

— She doesn't write, Helena says. But I could imagine. I saw the photographs.

— Maybe my photographs, he says.

— Maybe.

— It's my job to show the world, he says. But I cannot do it. Not really. I can photograph this man with the table on his head. But you must listen to him. You must see him every day. Not one picture in a magazine. Not twenty seconds on TV. And smell the smell of the rubbish and of the smoke and the dust. And then perhaps you begin to understand something.

She goes to the window and stands, looking out.

He says:

— But what does it mean, understand something? I was there a long time and I understand nothing.

She stands.

— You know what I mean? he says.

— When I go to sleep at night I think of her there, she says. When I wake up in the morning the first thing I think about is her. I sometimes feel, she says, that I'm not living in London but over there. In those bombed-out streets and collapsed houses. With the fear and the cold and the hunger. And then I tell myself: You pampered idiot. What do you know about it? What do you know?

She turns round.

She says:

— After that it's hard to get through the day.

He has broken the cigarette in two and is picking at the tobacco that has fallen on the table.

She says:

— It seems absurd to be here in my comfortable flat trying to write a book about a dead artist hardly anyone has heard of when all that is happening over there.

He sweeps the tobacco off the table with his hand.

— Absurd, she says, but what else is there to do?

— Let me tell you something, he says. Alice also feels like that.

— What do you mean?

— She feels that her life is meaningless. She often say.

— How can you say that?

— She often say, he says.

— That her work with these orphans is meaningless?

— You have to be there to understand, he says. There is unending stream of orphans there. Unending. Every child has lost at least one parent, often the two. And until recently everyone crazy. Driven crazy by the conditions. The Feds crazy with fear and with the drink and the drugs they take to forget their fear. The people crazy with fear and hating of the Feds and of the Chechen fighters and their new jihadist allies. And the aid workers crazy with fear and with the thought that nothing they do is any use and they have given their lives for a completely hopeless case. Now the followers of Kadyrov pretend everything fine. But is not fine. Is a gangster state, standing up by Putin. Is hollow. Everything gone. Even the last thing the Chechens had, when everything else gone, their dignity, their pride, that gone too. All the fighting for nothing. All the disappearances. All the tortures. For gangster state.

She says:

— Of course I read Tolstoy. *Hadji Murat.* When Alice first went out there. The opening image of the noble thistle, cut down by the farmer's blade, and then how the image returns at the end, when Hadji Murat is cut down on the island in the sodden fields. The indifference to human life of both the Tsar and the Imam who is fighting him, and of the innate nobility of the mountain people. And now you are telling me there is no more nobility. Ten years of Russian slaughter has destroyed a civilisation.

He is silent.

— But there are still children to look after, she says, sitting down opposite him again.

— They are wild children, he says. You give them love and they steal from you. They torture each other. They kill any animal they come across. How can you give them love?

— She would rather be there though than here, she says, where nothing happens and whatever you do seems to be of no importance.

— Perhaps she thinks it is of importance, he says.

— She told you that?

— She told me about your work, he says. She was proud.

— You're having me on, she says.

— Pardon me?

— When did she ever talk to you about my work?

— About your painter that you write about.

— Bonnard?

— No. The one you write about now.

— Cornell?

— Yes.

— How does she know I'm writing about him?

He is silent.

— She told you?

He nods.

— I don't believe you, she says.

He shrugs.

— I must have written to her about him, she says. I no longer know whether I'm writing to her in my head or on the page.

It's all the same anyway, since I get nothing back from her.

He is busy putting the remains of the shredded cigarette in his pocket.

— What did she say? she asks.

— She said he is weirdo.

— He's not a weirdo, she says.

He shrugs, picks a leaf of tobacco off the table and puts it in his pocket.

— Is it your word or hers?

— Pardon me?

— Weirdo. Is it your word or hers?

— Mine I think. Perhaps her.

— I wouldn't have devoted several years of my life to a weirdo, she says.

— I'm sorry.

— If she thinks that she can't have much sense of who I am, she says.

— I'm sorry, he says again.

— I'll have to explain to you, she says. If you're interested, that is.

— Of course, he says.

— There were strange things about him, she says, but when you compare him to real outsider artists you see at once that he was different.

— Outsider?

— People in asylums. Or who should have been in asylums. People like Adolf Wölfli and Henry Darger.

— I do not know, he says.

— Wölfli was a Swiss farm labourer who was arrested for child molestation and ended up in a psychiatric hospital, where he created an amazing oeuvre of over twenty-five thousand texts, drawings, collages and musical compositions, a kind of imaginary autobiography. Darger was a hospital porter in Chicago who lived in a rented room and when he died they found these enormous paintings in his room, forming a vast epic made up of thousands of images, recounting the adventures of a group of little girls with skirts and penises pursued by adult male hunters. He traced images from magazines and coloured them in, and they have a dreamy beauty about them and a sense of panorama that reminds me of Chinese scrolls, but that is all purely accidental. At heart this too is fantasy art, driven by obscure compulsions of which the artist is hardly aware. That is *really* weird.

She stops.

He says:

— I'm sorry.

— Don't apologise, she says. How could you know? Besides, Cornell had something of that. But only something. How he differs from those artists is what really interests me.

— Yes, he says.

— I tried to explain that to Alice, she says. But I doubt if she paid attention.

— Yes, he says.

— I'm sorry if I snapped at you, she says.

— No problem, he says.

## A Foul Mood

— I'm in a foul mood today, the old lady says.

— Why? Helena asks her.

— It's one of those days. I can't settle down to anything. People keep interrupting me. And I just don't have the right head on.

— Am I one of those people?

— Of course not, dear. You know you're always welcome.

— Shall I make some tea?

— Do, dear.

— I'm going to have to climb onto the table to get at the sugar.

— Climb away, the old lady says.

When they are finally settled with the tea before them, Helena says: — I have someone staying with me, did you know?

— I heard.

— A Czech journalist. From Chechnya.

— He's a friend of Alice's?

— He came here because of her.

— What's his name?

— Ed.

— Ed?

— That's what he said.

— Is that a Czech name?

– I suppose it's short for Edward.

– Is Edward a Czech name?

– I think so. They spell it Edouard.

– I see, the old lady says.

– He said to call him Ed.

– Funny, the old lady says.

– That's what he said, Helena says.

– What's he like?

– I don't want him here, Helena says.

– I'm not surprised, the old lady says. You want to get on with your work.

– It's not just that.

– You don't like him?

– I just don't want him here.

– Then tell him to leave.

– He has nowhere else to go.

– He could go to a hotel.

– He doesn't have any money. He's looking for work.

– How long does he intend to stay?

Helena pours the tea. – Till he finds work, she says. He said one or two days.

– He worked for an English paper?

– He's a photographer. Freelance I think. But they've just thrown him out.

– Out of Czechoslovakia?

– No no. Out of Chechnya.

– Why?

– Who knows?

– He hasn't told you?

– Not really, no. He probably doesn't know himself.

— Where does he want to go?

— Wherever they want to send him, I suppose.

— Is it easy, getting that sort of job? the old lady asks. How old is he?

— Thirty-five. Forty. Maybe a bit more.

— He has a family?

— There's a wife, I think. And a son.

— In Chechnya?

— No no. In the Czech Republic.

— Why doesn't he go back there?

— I didn't ask.

— You don't ask much, do you?

— No, Helena says.

— What does Alice say about him?

— You know she never writes. Maybe she does and letters don't get through. Phones don't work most of the time.

— She didn't warn you?

— No.

— Did he bring news of her?

— Yes. She's all right, it seems.

— They were close?

— I didn't ask.

— Lovers?

— I didn't ask.

— You know, dear, the old lady says, the advantage of being my age is that you can ask anything you like. You just wait and see.

Helena pours herself another cup of tea.

— Why don't you bring him up one of these days? The old lady says.

— So you can ask him yourself?

— You can leave us alone if it embarrasses you, the old lady says.

— And leave him in your clutches?

— You know you can trust me.

— I know I can't.

— Why not?

— For all the reasons you've given, Ruth. You think your age gives you the right to say whatever you like.

— I wouldn't do anything to embarrass you, Ruth says.

— Oh yes you would, Helena says.

She drinks down her tea and stands up. — I've got to go, she says.

— There's a family moving into the empty flat, the old lady says. Have you heard?

— Oh?

— Betsy told me.

— And?

— A young couple with a child. From Scotland.

— I hope they're quiet, Helena says.

— I'll let you know if I hear anything more, the old lady says.

Helena starts to bring the tea things to the sink.

— Leave, the old lady says. I'll do it later.

— Why should you? I don't want to add to your bad mood.

— Oh, that's quite passed away.

Helena picks up the old lady's cup.

— Leave, leave, the old lady says. It's nothing. And you won't forget, will you? Bring him up before he goes.

— When have I ever not done what you asked? Helena says.

– Umpteen times, the old lady says.

– Really?

– I've even got some whiskey here if he doesn't drink tea.

– He drinks tea all right, Helena says.

– You never know with these journalists, the old lady says.

# The Hands of Orlac

*Sometimes I'm tempted to throw away all I've written so far and start again, write quite a different kind of book, in the first person perhaps. Or write it in the third person but like a novel, with more freedom to go where a critical study could not go. Only then, I think, will I be able to get as close to Joseph Cornell as I feel I need to.*

*But then I remember that I have been here before, have entertained this idea, but quickly discarded it.*

*Why did I do that?*

*Because — I think — I sense that he himself never used the first person. In his notebooks he wrote a great deal about his daily doings and even his thoughts and impressions — I will come to that — but you feel, reading these, that he is essentially passive: life happens to him. Not even to him. There is no 'him' for life to happen to, in a sense. He is an absence, beyond speech. Before and after it. To make him the centre of a narrative would be to distort him even more than would writing a conventional critical study. He was never at the centre. Always at the side. If he was anywhere.*

*Yet he is not a man incapable of speech. After all, he talks to his brother, to his mother, to his artist friends, to his fellow Christian Scientists. Talks, in a way, in his notebooks, to himself.*

*It's true that as he grows older dialogue turns more and more into monologue. His friends and acquaintances all commented on this. At the end of his life, when he was living alone in the house on Utopia Parkway, he would talk on the phone to any of his friends who was prepared to listen. 'He would* talk for hours on end. I would get up and make myself some supper,' one of them recalls. 'Every now and again I would pick up the phone and make some sort of noise, so that he knew there was someone at the other end. He just kept going.'

Very like Glenn Gould, whose friends said the same thing about his phone calls towards the end of his life.

Today, no doubt, both of them would be diagnosed as suffering from a mild form of Asperger's Syndrome. But how far does that get us? We impose a term on an individual and imagine that explains him or her. I want to forget about labels. I want to find a way of writing about him without falsifying as I write.

So, he can speak, but not like other people. Or not quite like other people. But could we not say that of all of us? Do we not feel that language is really what others have? Never what we have?

Or is that just me, because of who I am, the product of my upbringing, my parents, my sister?

No need to find an answer. I am drawn to him anyway, for whatever reason.

Was there a time when one might have called his relations to language and to other people normal?

His letters home from school seem normal enough. Any fairly well-off child in America in the first decades of the twentieth century, writing from his private school, might have written them. Was it the death of his father, when he was sixteen, and his realisation that from then on he would be the one to look after his sick brother and helpless mother, the realisation that in time his two sisters would marry and move away (they did), leaving him with his sick brother and his mother in the house in Flushing until the end of time — was it this that brought about the change? Or was it his mother's extreme bourgeois rectitude, her intolerance of anything that would 'lower the tone', as she would have put it, combined with an innate coarseness of *spirit and an ineradicable small-town snobbery (her grandfather, as she never ceased to tell anyone who would listen, had been an admiral, and there was even a street in his home town of Nyack named after him)? Or was it the realisation, very early on, that his brother would never be able to speak as other people spoke, to walk as others walked? We cannot know. We can only speculate. And ponder the fact that North America seems peculiarly to produce these enigmatic creatures with the sign of speechlessness hung about their necks — Bartleby, Emily Dickinson, Glenn Gould, Bobby Fischer. The flip side of its dominant strain, the relentless pursuit of worldly goods, the emphasis on surfaces, the lack of history — leading, in a few isolated cases, to a stubborn refusal to take part: I would prefer not to.*

*What to do when you suddenly find yourself, in your teens, lacking the ability that seems to come naturally to others, to speak, to take your place in the group? In Cornell's case, what you do in the first instance is to use your feet. Like the protagonists of another of America's stricken geniuses, Edgar Allan Poe, he takes to wandering the streets of the big city. He treads the pavements of Manhattan to sell the cloth he is employed to sell on leaving school, and in his lunch hour and on his days off he stops to browse in the second-hand bookstalls and junk shops that were to be found everywhere in those days, or to stop and have a cake and a bottle of pop as he stares out of the window of a café at the crowds surging past outside. He walks by the sea near his house in Queens and picks debris off the shore, just as he buys what others have discarded in the rubbish-dumps and second-hand stores of Manhattan: old books, old records, reels of silent films, old photograph albums, old toys and trinkets, clay pipes, ships in bottles, whatever takes his fancy and he can afford. And so, as well as his legs, he starts to use his hands: to pick up a record of Caruso singing, a book of Max Ernst prints, a Victorian crystal ball which, when shaken, produces a sudden snow-storm to cover a miniature landscape or half-clothed maiden trapped inside. He walks through Manhattan gazing at the girls in their summer dresses, the waitresses in the tea-shops in their starched aprons, the cinema ticket salesgirls in their brightly lit booths, as enticing as the flickering films within, and he walks along the seashore, collecting stones and armfuls of seaweed and driftwood.*

*Across the world, in Austria, at the same time, 1924 (Cornell was twenty-one), the film director Robert Wiene was busy transferring a popular* roman noir *called* The Hands of Orlac *into the new medium (Cornell would become a great collector of silent movies, often coming across surprising treasures in dustbins, the man to contact if you wanted information or even rare footage — it was typical of him that those who so contacted him usually knew nothing about his reputation as an artist): A pianist loses his hands in an accident and a new pair is transplanted by a radical surgeon. Unfortunately the hands had previously belonged to the notorious strangler, Vasseur, and the consequences are predictable. The pianist (the great Conrad Veidt) gives up music and takes to strangling girls instead. The film was so popular it was remade in 1935 and again in 1960. Malcolm Lowry's hero in* Under the Volcano *is obsessed by the Spanish version,* Las Manos de Orlac, *posters for which crop up everywhere in his Mexican nightmare.*

*Seven years after Robert Wiene's effort, in Germany this time, a director of genius put on the screen another story of a man who lets his hands do his talking for him. Fritz Lang's* M *is the story of a paedophile and serial killer, played by Peter Lorre, who only kills because, when the need comes upon him, his hands cannot hold back. Before he kills he feels the urgent need to whistle, and what he whistles is the tune from Grieg's* Peer Gynt *suite, 'In the Hall of the Mountain King'. He does not speak. He is a loner, with no-one to speak to. Only at the end of his trial by the criminal underworld does he utter the words: 'Who knows what it's like to be me?', and Lang's film is so unsettling precisely because each of us, sitting alone in the darkness of the cinema, knows that M could be us.*

*If you cannot speak then it seems to be a law of nature that your body* will speak for you. Freud said as much in his very first psycho-analytical work, Studies on Hysteria, which he co-wrote with his colleague Joseph Breuer: 'Her painful legs,' he writes of one patient, 'began to "join the conversation" during our analysis.' And all the case studies in that book and in the many that followed merely elaborate on that: 'Her painful legs began to "join the conversation".'

Had circumstances been different Cornell could have become the Peter Lorre character, M, or one of Freud's patients. As it was, circumstances decreed that he become an artist. But a strange kind of artist. One who would create nothing, invent nothing – for creation and invention are after all ways of talking with pen or brush. Instead, he became an artist who merely put together what already existed. Because his mouth is gagged, we might say, he puts his hands to work.

He began with collage, alerted to the possibility by the chance discovery in a second-hand bookstall of Max Ernst's book of prints, La Femme 100 têtes. From the first his collages are unique and remarkable. In one an old schooner (memories perhaps of his admiral ancestor) is afloat in calm seas. But instead of an aft sail it carries an enormous white rose, within which a spider has spun a delicate web. The juxtaposition of rose and sail and rose and spider is less Surrealist than Blakean. But nothing quite means what it says here. The fine lines of the spider's web, which suggest that the rose is sick, echoes the ship's ropes and tackle, while the rich bloom of the rose, here figuring as a sail, suggests lassitude and torpor, and hints that the boat is not in calm seas but is actually becalmed. The image is so troubling precisely because of these multiple ambiguities achieved simply by the combination of a good eye, a deft hand and a genius for juxtaposition.

Three years later, in 1934, Cornell produced a less striking but even more remarkable collage. He had long been fascinated by depictions of the heavens, and in his wanderings had picked up three books by Camille Flammarion, one of the most successful nineteenth-century popularisers of astronomy, whose books teemed with marvellous colour plates, many dating back to the sixteenth and seventeenth centuries. 'Clipped illustrations from each of these books made their way into the artist's astronomy files, along with a battered copy of Les Etoiles,' writes Kirsten Hoving in her wonderful book on Cornell and astronomy. For the 1934 collage he takes the reproduction of the constellation Boötes, the Herdsman or Ploughman, originally published in Bayer's Uranometria. He hand-colours the figure's tunic and adds a cardboard box into which it seems Boötes is placing his right foot, and a breadbox containing a loaf in the upper right-hand corner. As Hoving explains: 'Irrational as these minor manipulations may seem, they demonstrate how carefully Cornell considered his subject. According to one of the legends of Boötes' origin in the sky, Ceres, the goddess of agriculture, was so pleased with his invention of the plough that she asked Jupiter to place him among the stars in gratitude. Another story explains that Boötes is the guardian of Ursa Major, the Great Bear, and of Taurus, the Bull. Bayer pictures Boötes in these roles, holding a crook and sickle and wearing his signature boots. Further underlining the constellation's association with agriculture is a sheaf of wheat to the right of the figure. In his collage, Cornell went a step further, turning the wheat into the loaf of bread in the box at the upper right. Moreover, in Cornell's version Boötes places his boot into a box, perhaps signifying the constellation Mons Menales, the Mountain of Menalus, on which Boötes stands in later atlases, including Bode's Uranographia of 1801, illustrated in Flammarion's Etoiles.'

Hoving also points out that while the boxes serve as visual puns for objects (breadbox, shoebox), they 'contrast the concept of containment with the limitless expanse of outer space', reinforcing this by the deployment of two different perspectival schemes enclosed in the one space. The scheme used to create the illusion of the three-dimensional cube in the depiction of the boxes clashes with the two-dimensional grid-lines of the celestial map. Hoving reads this as an indication that Cornell wants us to grasp the fact that we cannot *really conceive the limitlessness of the heavens. 'These little boxes,' she says, 'not only act as metaphors for the limitations of Renaissance geometrical perspective systems in depicting a boundless universe, but they also symbolize the limitations of human knowledge when facing the four-dimensional complexities of a universe predicated on a continuum of space and time.'*

*As so often happens, though, with even the best scholars, Hoving misses what seems to me a key ingredient in the collage: its wit. There is something odd, even ridiculous, in the great figure of Boötes with his foot stuck in a cardboard box. It's like a scene from a comic film in which the giant pursuer gets his foot stuck in a box and cannot move as his tiny victim scuttles away. The wit lies in the fact that the mythical figure from the skies has his foot trapped in a very real box, yet the box is no more real or unreal than the figure, it only seems more real to us because it is drawn, unlike Boötes himself, according to Renaissance perspective. We laugh at our own initial response just as we laugh at those 1913 collages of Picasso which shift continuously from precise perspectival realism to two-dimensionality. Our laughter stems from the recognition forced upon us by the artist that both modes are conventions, ways of rendering the world in two dimensions. But our laughter is also a response to the sudden awareness this brings that all our ways of conceiving of or talking about the world and ourselves are dependent on imposing arbitrary grids upon a fluid reality. As we look the world shifts under our feet.*

*Soon Cornell began to feel that collage alone did not give his hands (and legs) enough work to do. He looked into the junk-shop windows and he saw Victorian boxes filled with knick-knacks; he saw old ships' trunks and he remembered his admiral ancestor; he began to hoard three-dimensional objects — clay pipes, battered dolls, globes — as well as cheap prints and illustrations cut out of books, and he began to feel that they too needed to be manipulated, given new homes. So he walked and gazed and collected and began to make his shallow wooden boxes, his very own sailors' trunks for his own solitary voyages.*

*But though everyone is a bit odd and Cornell's predecessors and contemporaries in the realm of making detritus good again — Picasso, Duchamp, Schwitters — were no paragons of bourgeois respectability, Cornell was something else. Unlike them he had no idea of how to live in the world. Obsessed by a young woman selling cinema tickets in her well-lit booth, one day, after steeling himself, he bought her a bunch of flowers and, coming up to the booth in which she worked, suddenly thrust them at her and hurried away. She screamed at the sudden apparition and the manager, lurking nearby, ran out and tackled the retreating stranger, bringing him crashing to the ground. Many years later, obsessed this time by a young waitress, Joyce Hunter, who worked in one of the coffee-bars he haunted, he befriended her, invited her home, and gave her some of his boxes. Encouraged, she asked him for money, and, when he demurred, returned with her boyfriend and stole a number of boxes from the artist's ever-open garage. Apprehended by the police, she confessed, but Cornell refused to press charges. A few weeks later she was found strangled in her sordid bedsitter. Cornell mourned her passing and went on communing with her spirit, as with that of his dead brother and mother, to the end of his life.*

*Here he is, then, his beloved brother dead, the mother he could neither bear nor do without, dead, Joyce Hunter, dead, sitting all day in the kitchen of the empty house, wrapped in his old dressing-gown, by the open door of the lit oven. He hardly sleeps, or perhaps it would be more accurate to say that he hardly wakes, for he seems to exist in a state of permanent half-sleep. All who come to see him comment on the ghostly pallor of his skin and the sense of terminal depression that emanates from him like a smell. The energy that moved the hands to make the boxes and fill them with mysterious life has long gone. Or perhaps he made them for his brother and for the women who stirred his heart, and now Robert is dead and he is too weary even to go out, there is no longer any need of them. Or perhaps he made them for his mother, either to show her that he too was really worth something or to try to estab-*

lish his independence from her, or both, and now she is dead there is no longer any need for them. He will go on living in the house they shared for half a century, with its splendidly Cornelian address, that combination of the other-worldly and the down to earth, 571 Utopia Parkway, in Flushing, but around him the world has changed. The city has caught up with Flushing and Manhattan itself no longer has the plethora of junk-shops, flea-markets and second-hand book and record shops that once held him in thrall. Fame and recognition have never meant anything to him. For decades he has waged a covert vendetta against all who wished to collect his work, fearing perhaps that by doing so they would in some way be collecting him as well, and was once overheard by Robert Motherwell saying of a dealer: 'That so-and-so is too interested in selling my work.' So what is there to do but invite beautiful young women to tea, let Leila Hadley do what Leila Hadley evidently enjoys doing, and wait for the end?

## It Seems That They Mourn in Silence

They are sitting on a bench by a copse on Hampstead Heath looking north over Highgate Ponds.

She says:

— I've read so many books on Chechnya since Alice went out there that I think I've reached saturation point. I just can't bear to read any more. I've read histories of the region from the Middle Ages to the present. I've read Pushkin and Lermontov and Tolstoy on the Caucasus and everything Anna Politikovskaya ever wrote about it. I've read online accounts by political analysts in Western think-tanks and popular accounts in paperback of the Breslan and Moscow theatre hostage-taking and I just feel sick when I think about it. Is there no end to the horrors? To the idiocy and greed of men? Their sadism and indifference? Does it have to be like that?

He is silent.

She says:

— Does it have to be like that?

— You see, he says, if the Russians give independence to Chechnya then every ethnic minority in Russia will want independence. Even Gorbachev could not allow it.

— You believe that?

— I'm not a politician.

— But you believe it?

— Maybe.

— And would that be such a bad thing? she asks. Independence for the ethnic minorities?

— There are always Russians mixed up with them. Like Serbs in Bosnia.

— In Chechnya?

— Of course in Chechnya. In the old people's homes they are nearly all Russian. The Chechens have family that will take care of them. But there are many Russians in Chechnya that want to live quiet lives, but they have been victims of the Feds too, and often more than the Chechens. The Russian politicians cannot give in to minority demands.

— It's the disparity between the language of politicians and what actually happens to people that makes me despair, she says. The politicians mouth their platitudes and this is what it leads to: people dropped into pits to die of cold and starvation, the murder of innocent children in a school thousands of miles away, soldiers haggling with mothers over the price of their sons' corpses, the gunning down of journalists in the middle of Moscow.

He is silent.

— How can we go on with our work knowing this kind of thing is happening in the world? she says. And yet we must. Otherwise we'd go mad. But it makes us mad to repress it too, doesn't it?

He is silent.

— I suppose we could all be like Alice and you, she says. And do something about it.

— I do nothing, he says.

— Aren't your photographs something?

He laughs. — Maybe once I think so, yes, he says.

— And now?

He says:

— You see, perhaps it is the West that was mad. For two hundred years. Enlightenment. Human rights. No-one heard of these things before in history and in China and Russia and Saudi Arabia and Uganda they do not know what it means and do not want to know. It is for them like a sickness that will pass. They almost feel sorry for Europe and America because all this baggage means that these countries will sink in economy and then in power. It is already happening. In China and Russia the leaders do not want lectures from the West. They laugh. They are not interested in human rights. They are not interested in democracy. Why should they be? It is not in their history. It is not in their interest.

— That's a pretty depressing view of things, she says.

— Maybe, he says.

— You laugh at people like Alice?

— No I don't laugh, he says. I admire.

— Well then.

He is silent.

She says:

— I sit here on the Heath and my heart lifts when I see the ponds gleaming down there and the curve of the hill above them and the spire of Highgate Church peeping out among the trees. How can I be living in the same world as the one Anna Politikovskaya writes about? The same one Alice works in every day? The same one you photograph?

— It's the same world, he says.

— I know it is, she says. There is no other. But it's hard to take, isn't it? Or perhaps you don't think so?

— A person cannot understand, he says. That is the mistake you make. The first thing you learn as a journalist is that you cannot understand. Your job is to report, not understand. If you think you understand you become a bad journalist.

— But can you even know what to report if you don't understand?

— You follow your instincts, he says.

— And they don't let you down?

— Of course, he says. But not as much as the belief that you can understand. And sometimes you get lucky. You know what I mean?

— You uncover something important?

— Important, he says. That is a big word.

— How do you want to put it? Significant?

— Maybe, he says.

— But how can you even sense that it's significant if you don't have a vision of the whole?

— You smell it, he says.

They sit.

She asks:

— How did you get into it?

— Into it?

— What you do.

— I wanted to be a wildlife photographer, he says. I love animals. I went to Africa to photograph the beautiful creatures there. And then I saw what was happening to them. And I stopped being a wildlife photographer.

— Is it worse than Chechnya?

— Animals do not know what is happening, he says. They do not understand.

— And the Chechens do?

— They can choose to fight or to submit. Or they can make plans to get out. And if they cannot do that at least they can speak. They can wail.

— And animals?

— It seems that they mourn in silence, he says.

They sit.

She says:

— Like my artist.

— Pardon me?

— Cornell. In the photos I showed you.

— Ah, he says. Perhaps there is the quality of the wounded animal. You see it in Chechnya also. After the tearing of the hair and the lamentations, silence. Some do never speak again.

They sit.

She says:

— Shall we move?

They get up. They go down through the long grass towards the ponds and the people and the dogs.

— Can we go another way? he asks.

She veers abruptly. — This way then.

They walk along the side of the hill, away from the ponds.

— Tell me about Alice, she says.

— I told you.

— More.

— What?

— I don't know. Tell me.

— She has become thin.

— She was always thin.

— Very thin.

— There isn't enough to eat?

— That is true, everybody is thin. Except the Kadyrovsky. But she is different.

— She's ill?

— I don't know.

— There are doctors?

— Some. When you can get.

— She drives herself too hard?

— Pardon me?

— She works too much?

— Too much? No. It is always too much.

They walk through the trees.

— Tell me how she lives, she says. What kind of place she lives in.

— She has lived in many rooms in the time I have known her, he says. But it is always the same room. She has a rug and a cover for the bed. A blue pot. Always the colourful rug and the bed covering and the blue pot.

— What kind of pot?

— A jug. You know what I mean? Dark blue. Glazed. It is an Arab jug. Very different from what we have in the Czech Republic, and you know we are famous for jugs.

— And the rug?

— It is colourful. From Asia somewhere. And over the bed the colourful covering. Also from Asia.

— She would give you coffee?

— Yes. Always coffee.

They walk. Under their feet the dry earth is cracking.

— And her hair? she asks. Is it short? Grey?

— Yes, he says.

— Yes what?

— Pardon me?

— Yes short or yes grey.

— The two. Not like when I first knew her.

— We won't go that way, she says. It leads into Kenwood and too many people.

They turn up a path in the woods.

— How long have you known her? she asks.

— A long time, he says. From when I first went. Then I did other things. In other parts of the world. And then I came back to Chechnya when the second war was ending. And she was still there. With more grey in the hair. And then she had become much thinner.

— And the children?

— Ah, the children, he says.

## I'm the Lady

On her way down from the old lady's she finds a child standing by the open door of the flat that has been empty for some months.

— Good morning, she says.

The child stands by the open door and stares up at her.

She bends down. — You don't know me, she says. But I too live here.

The child goes on staring, not moving.

— What's your name? Helena asks.

The child goes on staring, mouth slightly open.

— Have you just moved in? Helena asks.

The child goes on staring.

— Is your mother in?

She straightens, calls through the open door: — Hello? Anyone in?

She says to the child:

— Where's your mother?

Nothing.

— Is she in?

Still nothing.

— Will you go and call her?

— Why? the child asks suddenly.

— I just want to say hello. I'm the lady from the flat below.

— Do you want to speak to my mother?

— Yes please.

The child does not move.

— Don't worry if she's busy, Helena says.

The child puts a finger into her mouth without taking her eyes off her.

— Never mind, Helena says, I'll call another time. Tell your Mummy the lady from the flat below called to say hello.

The child feels around with her finger in the back of her mouth.

— Will you remember that?

The child takes her finger out of her mouth and examines it.

— Never mind, Helena says.

She starts down the stairs, stops, turns and waves.

The child stands in the doorway, her finger back in her mouth, staring after her.

She turns again and goes on down the stairs.

## I Don't Know How to Go On

– I don't know how to go on, she says.

– Why? Tom says.

– I don't know what I'm doing any more.

– You're writing a book about Joseph Cornell, he says.

– Am I?

– Like you've written a book about Monet and a book about Bonnard. Remember?

– I don't know, she says. It just won't fall into place. Perhaps because time didn't seem to figure in his life as it does in most people's, and books, or at least the books I write, tend to develop in time and to be to a certain extent about development over time.

He is silent.

– I suppose I feel closer to Monet's and Bonnard's acceptance of time, she says, to their building of time into their pictures, so to speak, rather than denying it altogether or seeking to fly above it, as Cornell does in both his life and his art.

– But he lived in time, like you and me, Tom says. He died.

– I don't want to do a life, she says. It's been done. Very well. And I don't want to do a critical study. That's been done too. By dozens of good scholars.

– Then what do you want to do?

– I don't know.

– Think, he says.

She is silent.

He says:

– Those aren't the alternatives. Either pure biography or pure art criticism. You wrote about Bonnard's relations with Marthe, didn't you? Marthe in the bath, Marthe in the bathroom. Was that about the life or the art? And what about Berger's Picasso? It's about his art, isn't it, but in order to be about that it has to be about a lot of things that aren't pure art, that aren't even art at all.

– I don't like that book, she says.

– But you go along with the principle?

– I suppose to some extent I do, she says.

– Well then.

She is silent, sipping her coffee.

She says:

– I've thought about all that. Of course I have. But I'm still troubled. Cornell's boxes enclose a magical past. Many of them. A past he knew never existed. But one he imagined with intensity, as much intensity as his beloved Novalis and Gerard de Nerval. Those ballerinas never coming down to earth, those Renaissance princes forever young, those snowflakes without substance falling onto an earth without mass – and then the passions he developed for young women, for starlets who never grow old and waitresses in their little aprons – there is something so naked about the unconscious that generates these things that there's the danger of falling into the obvious and the embarrassing. But we can't ignore them either, or at least I can't, though the best books on him do. There's something a little too close to the bone about them, a lack of wit in their deployment, that makes me uncomfortable, as I'm never uncomfortable with Duchamp or Schwitters, say, or van Gogh. Yet there's something else in him, something quite different, harder to get to grips with. A kind of controlled panic, which you see in the best of his works, or even in that very early collage of the schooner with the rose and cobweb sail — I respond to that. It's as strong as Blake's 'O rose thou art sick'. And then those late photos of him in the yard or in his study, ashen, empty — as I told you, that's what I want to get at, but I can't. As soon as I put something down I have the sense that I'm not writing about him any more, that he's evaded me, slipped away. And it's my fault.

She drains her cup.

— More? he asks.

— No thanks.

They sit.

— I think you've got to stalk it, he says.

— Stalk it?

— Yep.

— Like a prey?

— Uhuh. Pretend it's not there. Keep your ears open. Move away from it and then, when you feel it's letting down its guard, pounce.

— And how does my book get written?

— It gets written. Trust it.

— Thanks, she says.

— You don't like my advice?

— I think it's excellent advice. I just don't know how to apply it.

She pushes the cup away from her. — I'm sorry, she says. I don't even ask about your work any more.

— That's all right.

— How's it going?

— You don't have to ask.

— No. I want to.

— OK.

— So?

— It's going.

— About the two sisters?

He smiles at her.

— You're having me on, she says.

— Why should I do that?

— Because.

— Because what?

— To pay me back.

— Pay you back? What for?

— For meandering on about my failures.

— They're not failures.

— OK. Tell me.

— It's very simple, he says. There are two sisters. Living very far apart. Can't stop thinking about each other. After a while we're no longer sure which of them we're with. Is it A thinking about B or B thinking about A thinking about B or A thinking about B thinking about A thinking about B or —

— All right, she says. You've made your point.

— I'm enjoying it, he says.

— I've got to go, she says.

— Why not stay the night?

— No. I've got to go.

— Go on. You won't die.

— Don't be a bore, Tom.

— It'll help with your book.

— You must be joking, she says.

— It will, Lena. Really.

— I think I'll try more conventional means first, she says.

## Nothing to Do Except Die

He says:

— People used to say that if the corpse was not thrown out in five to seven days that was a good sign. It meant they had survived the torture of the first days and been sent to Kankala. But if they did not come out of the Federal jails in five to seven days you had to look for a corpse. The women in the family would stand in the road leading to the military base until the curfew, waiting for news. Often a go-between would come out and bargain over those still inside. Or for the corpses.

They stand back to let a group of cyclists pass.

He says:

— I asked the son of a man who had recently been handed back to the family, dead, what they did apart from hiding from the Feds. Because young men cannot just stay at home every day, just to show they are not militants. And he said to me: There is nothing to do except die.

They walk.

He says:

— Once I remember there was a crowd of women trying to get at the small food rations the Feds were handing out to them. They were cursing and fighting with each other over these rations. And spitting at each other. Because they had TB. So many people in Chechnya in those years had TB. And so they were trying to infect the others in this crowd with their disease, from rage or hoping that the healthy ones would get out of their way and they could take their rations. Can you imagine that? And a cordon of soldiers with automatic weapons trying to keep order among all these crazy women, not from sympathy with them but to make it possible to distribute the rations.

They walk.

He says:

— What is terrible is to see the way these proud people have been reduced to this, he says. To see how their independence and their dignity were crushed by the war and the brutality and the hunger. And all the rich Chechen businessmen and crooks in the West will not give one penny to help. And the same with the rest of the world. Not one penny. Not a voice in protest. Because you see, the West, they need Putin. They need his gas and his good will, so they shake their heads and do nothing.

— I think I read about the tubercular women spitting at each other in their queues for food in one of Politikovskaya's books, she says.

— Yes, she was with me that day, he says.

He lets her go ahead of him under a bridge.

They walk.

— Go on, she says.

He is silent.

— Tell me more, she says. You knew Politikovskaya?

— I have too many worries, he says. I do not want to talk about such things.

— That was our agreement, she says. You tell me about

Chechnya and Alice and I let you stay in the flat.

— I have too many worries, he says. I do not want to talk.

They walk.

— Please, she says. Tell me about Alice.

He stops.

He says:

— Helena, I do not understand you.

— You think I understand myself?

— Pardon me?

— Leave it, she says. We're almost home anyway.

# Round and Round

– Up here one breathes, Helena says.

– Oh, but you breathe down below as well, the old lady says.

The breeze sweeps the red and white check curtains out of the window and sets them waving frantically at anyone who cares to look up.

– Not in my flat, Helena says. Not at my desk. This book won't let me breathe. It's like a weight on my chest. All the time.

– You know, Ruth says, you have come up here and said exactly the same thing every year since I've known you.

– Have I?

– Yes you have.

– Really?

– Really.

– Then why don't I remember?

– It's like childbirth, Ruth says.

Helena laughs.

– Believe me, Ruth says. I've given birth. Twice.

– I know, Helena says. But I still don't quite believe you.

– I should have recorded what you said, Ruth says. Then I could play it back to you.

– I'll get you a machine, Helena says.

— That's a good idea, Ruth says. Then next time you deny it I can play it back to you.

— I'm trying to imagine it, Helena says. I think even if I heard myself saying it I still wouldn't be able to believe it. I'd think: No, it was different then.

— But you'll know it wasn't really.

— Will I? Helena says. I wonder.

— What you've got to do, Ruth says, is ask yourself why it feels like that.

— You think I haven't done that?

— Well tell me then.

— Perhaps deep down I don't really want to do it, Helena says. Perhaps I feel it's violating him in some way to obtrude on what he wanted hidden. He was so jealous of his privacy. So ambiguous about whether what he was making was a way of talking to the world or to himself.

— Couldn't it be both? Ruth asks. We none of us have clear or unambiguous reasons for what we do, you know.

— Or perhaps I just haven't found the form I want, Helena says. A form that would allow me to say what I felt I wanted to say about him without it turning into something else in the very act of saying it.

— I don't understand what you mean, Ruth says.

— If I write a conventional critical study, Helena says, I will have left out the pain and desolation of much of the life, which is not only the soil from which the art springs, but what the art is so often about. On the other hand to highlight that is to risk turning him into a 'case' and to detract from the extraordinary quality of the work. If I write, as I've occasionally been tempted to do, a portrait of him 'from the inside', I'm left with the feeling that I'm furnishing him with an 'inside' which is not there. That's the hardest thing to get round. Perhaps one can't. I just have to let it go.

— I still don't understand, Ruth says. You go too fast for me.

— I don't either, Helena says. I only know when I'm frustrated with the other approaches the temptation wells up in me to try to enter his world, to try and take the reader into his world, but then I immediately feel that it's as misleading as all the others. For what is 'his world'? And how do I have access to it? And then I'm overwhelmed with the feeling that he has no inside to enter, to convey to others, or rather, his inside is made up of feelings and impressions which never crystallise into anything that could say 'I' or be designated as a 'he'.

The old lady is distracted by the curtains blowing suddenly back into the room.

— I just go round and round in circles, Helena says.

— Do you, dear? the old lady says.

— Tom thinks I just need to write it, Helena says. He thinks if I just keep at it something will emerge.

— He should know, Ruth says. He's a professional writer.

— That's the problem, Helena says. I don't know that I want to be a professional. Father always said: We're leaving you a little money so that neither of you will ever need to do what you don't feel it's right to do simply in order to survive.

— That's all very well, Ruth says, but you know you've got to communicate with your audience.

— It just means I don't have to write the book at any cost, Helena says. If I don't get it right I can just drop it.

— But you don't want to drop it, do you? Ruth says.

— No, of course not. Cornell attracted me in the first place because he obscurely spoke to something in me, and I want to do justice to both him and me.

— Then you will, Ruth says.

— But perhaps I can't, Helena says. I've got to face that. And in that case I feel very strongly that I shouldn't do something that does neither of us justice. I owe it to both of us.

— In that case, Ruth says, you should just turn to something else.

— I've been thinking that, Helena says.

— And have you something in mind?

— I've thought of writing the biography of a single work, Helena says. Perhaps of Blake's *Ghost of a Flea*.

— Now you're laughing at me, Ruth says.

— No, Helena says. I mean it.

— Blake painted something called *The Ghost of a Flea*?

— It's such a frightening and mysterious work, Helena says. According to Blake himself it was a direct transcription of a vision he had, of the flea as a repulsive being, half-man half-reptile, with a small head on a bull neck and a serpent-like tongue darting out between its lips, stalking across a heavily curtained room. It feels massive, overwhelming, yet it's a tiny painting. And, oddest of all, Blake uses gold leaf mixed with tempera, something one would have thought he'd reserve for a vision of goodness, not evil. To write its biography would be to drill into the heart of the late eighteenth and early nineteenth centuries, where, after all, our modern world was born, as well as into the heart of Blake himself, perhaps the greatest English artist since Anglo-Saxon times.

— I'm not sure I'd buy the book, Ruth says. It sounds frightful.

— It is frightful, Helena says. That's why I'd like to explore it.

— At my age, Ruth says, you don't really want to go searching for shocks. You get enough of them without that.

— I'd also thought of Magritte's *L'Assassin Menacé*, Helena says.

— Now you're showing off, Ruth says.

— No I'm not, Helena says. Just because you don't know the picture doesn't mean I'm showing off. And you wouldn't be frightened of this one. We see a room through a door open onto an antechamber. In the room a naked woman, obviously dead, lies on a couch.

— That's not frightening? Ruth says.

— Not really, Helena says. Not the way it's painted. It's as if the whole thing is a kind of distillation of gory thrillers of the twenties and thirties, but very much in inverted commas, from the title on, which is both the kind of title you'd find in such works and, when you say it aloud, a kind of game in which the first word morphs into the second, or the second transforms the first: L'a-ssa-ssin/Me-na-cé. Do you see?

— Well go on, Ruth says. Describe the rest of it.

— So, there's this naked woman, dead, lying on a couch. The assassin, at least one imagines it's him, a well-dressed man, stands in the middle of the room, ready to leave, his coat and hat on a chair next to his bag. He seems to have stopped, however, to listen to the gramophone, one hand in his trouser pocket, leaning with the other on a table near the door on which the gramophone sits, his ear cocked towards the giant horn, which is painted an unpleasant greenish colour. Outside, at a window in the rear centre, three men look into the room, behind them high mountains which rise up to the dark sky. In the antechamber, on either side of the door, two more men wait, one with a club in his hands, the other with a net, though whether they are the assassin's accomplices or have come to apprehend him, it is impossible to say, though the title suggests the latter.

— You do have a dark imagination, Ruth says.

— You have to realise this is a comic painting, Helena says. Comic because of the way all the men are dressed, in typical Magritte style, in suits and the two in the doorway with bowler hats, and because of the gramophone, which seems to cast a spell over the whole scene. Comic and magical and a little bit sinister.

— There you are, Ruth says.

Helena is silent.

Ruth says:

— Is your friend still there?

— My friend?

— From Chechnya.

— Yes, she says. He's still there.

— No sign of his going?

— No.

Ruth is silent.

— To come back to this book, Helena says. I should know what questions I'm asking at least. It's my fault if I don't.

— It's not your *fault*, Ruth says. It's just the way it is.

— Does it have to be like that?

— Probably, Ruth says.

— What does that mean?

— I'm only trying to help.

— You are helping, Helena says. You're being wonderful.

— Am I? Ruth says.

— Perhaps it's just age, Helena says. One does things in one's youth without thinking and they come off, but after a while that lovely innocence seems to vanish.

— But you can also do things later on which you would never have been able to do in your youth, Ruth says.

— I wish I could believe you, Helena says.

— You do believe me, Ruth says. That's why you keep on at it.

— That's not the reason, Helena says, it's more that I don't know how to do anything else.

— But you never write a book without believing in it, Ruth says. You're a determined woman. You always have been. As long as I've known you.

— You think I share a bit of Alice's determination, do you?

— I wouldn't know, Ruth says. I only know you. Her I get refracted through your hero-worship.

— You think I hero-worship her?

— Don't you?

— Plenty of determined people have got nowhere, Helena says.

— True.

— We look back at their lives and just find them pushy and ridiculous.

— Sometimes, Ruth says.

— So even if I am determined, who's to say I'm right?

— No-one.

— Well then?

— We never know, Ruth says. And I mean never. People

who die thinking they've achieved a great deal are later judged to have done nothing at all, while others who die feeling they've wasted their lives are later seen to have achieved wonders. But even those judgements aren't written in stone, are they? Another generation comes along and thinks just the opposite. The truth is, we can never know.

— Well then, Helena says.

— Well then nothing, Ruth says. We struggle along as best we can and try to do what we can. And that includes you.

— Thank you, Helena says.

— I mean it, Ruth says. I'm not saying it to cheer you up.

— I know you do, Helena says.

— So you'll just press on, Ruth says.

— You think so?

— I do, Ruth says. And at the end of it there'll be a book.

— That's what I fear, sometimes, Helena says.

— You fear you'll have a new book?

— I fear I'll have a new book I don't really believe in.

— That, Ruth says, is a chance you have to take.

## Short for Michaela

On the way down she comes face to face with the new occupants.

She says:

– Hello. I live on the ground floor, as I told your little girl.

– Oh?

– I'm Helena.

– I'm Amy. This is Mick.

– Hello, Mick.

– I hope we didn't make too much noise moving in.

– Not a sound. And the walls aren't all that great in this house. Lisa, who was here before you, used to tinkle away on the piano and sing at all hours of the day and night. It almost drove me crazy.

– We don't have a piano. But I'm afraid when this arrives it might be difficult for you.

– When's he due?

– She.

– She.

– December.

– Poor thing.

– Why?

– My sister's a December child. It meant her birthday and

Christmas tended to elide and she always felt she was missing out.

— Oh, Amy says, we'll make sure that doesn't happen.

— And when's your birthday, Mick?

The child stares up at her.

— October, her mother says.

— Ah, Helena says.

— Do you think Mick's a boy's name? the little girl asks.

— I do, actually.

— It needn't be. It's short for Michaela.

— I see.

— You must come and have coffee, Amy says. When Harry gets here.

— I'd love to.

— He's stayed in Glasgow. Trying to wrap things up there.

— I see.

— Will you? Come and have coffee?

— I'd love that, Helena says. And if there's anything I can do…?

— Thank you. It's just a question of time. And with Harry away I have to juggle with the move and Mick and work and all the rest of it.

— That's why I…

They stand on the landing.

— I have to go, Helena says. It was good to meet you.

— We'll have that coffee soon.

— Lovely.

— Go on then, Amy says to her daughter. You can see I haven't got any hands. Just take it out of my pocket.

# GC 44

He never put pen to paper to make a drawing, but he constantly did so to write — to confide to his notebooks, write to friends, scribble notes for himself for later inclusion in his extensive folders.

It is often difficult to tell what is fact, what is fantasy and what is vision in his voluminous writings. He writes to Pavel Tchelitchew, for example: 'The day I was visiting [the Planetarium] Hedy Lamarr was the lecturer and she spoke with a wonderful soft detachment that is her unique pictorial appeal.'

Too often he simply puts down the facts: 'Made lemon butter cream cake 2.00 a.m.' Or: 'Obsessive feeling of physical pressure (back and neck) & unsettled feeling (vacillation, etc.)' And too often he tries to capture a feeling of exaltation but succeeds only in being banal and sentimental: 'The "all over" feeling that makes of the incidental a never ceasing wonder and spectacle of the spiritual.' Often it just feels dead on the page, whatever it was like in real life: 'Overflow of the spirit — pure joy.' Sometimes the notes are simply intriguing: 'mirror-magic in cafeteria'.

The largest file he ever kept was the one he called GC 44. This refers to the year 1944, when, having given up work in a munitions factory, he found a job in a garden centre in Flushing, within cycling distance of his house — 'the most significant of all my explorations GC 44', he writes to Susan Sontag in 1966, '— not completely cabbalistic Garden Center 1944 where I took employment in a garden nursery "center" which became the hub of an infinite no. of journeys.' He was forty-one, but he lived those months *like the young Wordsworth in Grasmere — 'Bliss was it in that dawn to be alive.' He loved the cycle rides that reminded him of his childhood in Nyack, that took him far away from the newly built roads and houses to the seashore, there to forage for the driftwood, dried grasses and pebbles he could use for his boxes — 'mystical dream episodes of bicycle rides through lonesome landscapes' is how he describes it, 'beautiful country feeling through rural roads still unspoilt by developments... countless contacts with nature — the meadows surrounding the Lawrence homestead, in the opposite direction towards the water, unspoilt stretches through Bayside via Bell Avenue, unspoiled stretches of Bayside West.'*

*He felt that he had become the custodian of a dying way of life: 'Lawrence Farm, auction sign up... brought back wild asters and grasses a feeling of being a "custodian" of what is left of the original beauties of plant and grasses before complete oblivion.'*

*In September 1946 he writes: 'Up early (6) not very relaxed or rested. Yesterday working at anger very tense — afternoon anger released in spots. Decided to take short ride on bicycle not feeling like longer one — but autumnal zest of early morning wrought a magic of renewal — rising sun effects from clear weather midday rich and colourful — migrating birds scattered drifts heading South way up like specks against pink glow (remembered for magnificence of beauty at evening). Found as in a dream a pile of wood, box & films on spools in junk pile. Took them home and started again.'*

*Eleven days later: 'Sept. 26, 1946. Exaltation generally felt only on long bike rides came in overflowing measure before breakfast — clouds of moisture hang over fields around station — effects of light striking and shining through — now indistinct as though filled with smoke.*

*"heroic" smiling quality of Robert carrying (lunch, etc.): vanilla flip, vanilla syrup and cherry.'*

*He looked back to that time as to a golden age. The file includes his later comments, of which this one from 1950 is typical: 'The approaches to the sea* and water are no longer the idyllic and Elysian fields of five summers ago.'

But that too goes into the file. And one of his problems becomes how to organise it, how to bring out the riches he senses it contains. For he is aware that the period it covers was one of enormous emotional excitement for him — too much emotion, in fact, to be easily containable: ' — rapid overflow of experience... ever-opening paths leading ever further afield. Unbelievably rich cross-indexing (of experience) the ceaseless flow and interlacing of original experience.'

'Ever-opening paths leading ever further afield' — how to hold on to 'the ceaseless flow and interlacing of original experience'? How to hold on to it and not kill it in the process?

At one point he turned to a book that meant a great deal to him, particularly in this period of intense inner turmoil and of the powerful memories his cycle rides and working in the garden centre evoked of his childhood — Alain-Fournier's Le Grand Meaulnes, tellingly translated into English as The Wanderer. (Why have the French, who are not known for their children's books, nevertheless provided the English-speaking world with two of their best-loved books about childhood, Le Grand Meaulnes and Le Petit Prince? Is it because these have a kind of sentimentality which the English feel deprived of in their own sharper and more satirical and comic books for children, such as Alice in Wonderland and The Wind in the Willows?) 'The titles comprising the sep. category of this compilation might be likened to the chapter headings of an adventure or a mystery novel but one in which the sensational element is entirely missing. ("Le Grand Meaulnes" of A-F.)' This, as Lindsay Blair points out, 'led him to separate out some of the notes in "CG 44" under headings that would suggest separate episodes or journeys — "The Festival of Nature", "The Little Dancer", "The Floral Still-Life", "The House on the Hill", "The Old Farm".'

But these were vain endeavours, and right to the end of his life Cornell was still struggling to bring order into the jottings in this enormous file. For *the truth is that the only order he was capable of was the infinitely ambiguous one of his boxes; he was, after all, an artist, not a writer — albeit a very strange sort of artist. And though he found it difficult to recapture the heady excitement of 1944, while it lasted it fed into his boxes, just as the joy of making boxes he knew were good fed back into his life.*

*A page simply headed 'GC 44' captures the atmosphere of that time. He is looking back and recalling the thrill of gathering material and then making a box:*

*'the many trips made by bicycle gathering dried grasses of different kinds, the fantastic aspect of arriving home almost hidden on the vehicle by the loads piled high*

*'the transcendent experience of threshing in the cellar, stripping the stalks onto newspapers, the sifting of the dried seeds, then the pulverising by hand and storing in boxes.*

*'These final siftings were used for habitat (imaginative) boxes of birds principally owls. The boxes were given a coating of glue on the insides then the grass throw in and shaken around until all the sides had an even coating to give them the aspect of a tree-trunk or nest interior.*

*'Although used in the construction of objects the nights when the cellar was filled with the aroma of these acrid scents with all the good richness stored in them by afternoons under the hot autumnal sun, the subsequent rains and moistures, the dryings out again, etc., all this complements beautifully the House on the Hill. Then I was in the house on the Hill working like an herbalist or apothecary of old with these sweet scents in my own fashion. The discovery of making boxes so like a bird's own nest was inexpressibly satisfying in such a warm and redolent atmosphere.'*

*Cornell, who never felt at home in his own body or in his own house, makes his boxes as a nest for himself. Yet it is not exactly that the box is a nest, rather that the constructing of the box and the constructing of a nest, a home, become for him one and the same. This cuts across the dichotomy home/exile, so beloved of cultural commentators, and places the emphasis squarely on the* activity, the process *of making — that is the true home. (Develop)*

*And what of the mysterious 'House on the Hill', which appears so often in the folder and is invoked in this note? An entry for September 1944, copied in 1947 and typed up in 1948, thus attesting to its importance for Cornell, tells of a bicycle ride that day:*

'— *Misty — overcast — bike ride to Whitestone, unexpectedly after breakfast — discovered the shopping district of Whitestone — bakery for the first time (bread, jelly, doughnuts, cake, bought)*

'— *A vivid and powerful evocation of the 1932 canvassing visits (depression period) — recollection of the "flavour" of Whitestone when first known with its "backward aspect", removal of railroad branch — one seems to enter another world so quickly in these parts — the "house on the hill" must have come back too with remarkable vividness — with a recreative force —*

'— *One of the finest boxes (objects) ever made was worked out this day (completed or almost). The box of a white chamber effect with a "fountain" of green sand running. Shell, broken stem glass for receptacle. The Italian Girl in the house on the hill was evoked with an overwhelming sense of melancholy — momentarily — watching the sand run out and associating it to the house in the past as she had so used it a hundred years ago. A genuine evocation that can never be adequately put down in words. Completely natural.'*

*Was there a House on the Hill? Or was it just a house on a hill? What is this name, Malba House, that keeps cropping up in his notes in association with it? Is Malba the name of the 'Italian Girl' who, it is suggested, lived there 'a hundred years ago'? Was Cornell creating for himself a Big House to vie with that stumbled upon by the hero of Alain-Fournier's novel? A house that both exists and doesn't exist, that is both magical and mundane? Or was there a house and did he imagine its inhabitants? But then how come that he too seems to be an inhabitant, at work in the house as he was at work in his own cellar in Utopia Parkway, like a bird building a nest? For that seems to be the meaning of that enigmatic entry: 'Then I was in the house on the Hill working like an herbalist or apothecary of old with those sweet scents in my own fashion.' And what is the force of that opening 'then'? In another life? In the summer of 1944?*

*In 1947, like Krapp commenting on tape on past tapes, he writes in his journal about his re-reading of some of the GC 44 material. He actually entitles his note: 'The House on the Hill (Malba)', making it clear that it remained embedded in his imagination and his private mythology, taking its place among his beloved constellations: 'It — this house — now stands a lone surviving sentinel (from its vantage point) for all my chaotic treasure — a celestial repository.'*

*But a little lower down comes the sad confession: 'going through GC notes without enough enthusiasm to get into the spirit or catch up the thread noticed tonight'.*

## Not Even the Tiniest Chink

– I dreamed of Alice last night, she says to the old lady.

– And what did you dream?

– I dreamed I was standing in that street or square in Grozny. The one in the photograph that's always reproduced, with the ruined houses on either side stretching back into an empty distance and three people walking in single file across the rubble and the craters. I had a piece of paper in my hand with an address on it, but the streets were deserted and there was no-one to ask the way from. I dug about in my bag and found another piece of paper, with a rough map drawn on it, and arrows going this way and that all over it, but as I held it up to the light to try and understand how it related to my surroundings a gust of wind blew it from my grasp and it went dancing off down the street. I ran after it and stumbled over something and found myself lying in one of the craters made by the shells or bombs which make of this city something more like a waste land or a tip than anything else. I lay in the bottom of this small crater, and then I began to hear voices. The hole was full of people talking animatedly in a language I couldn't understand and I felt someone shaking me and realised all this had been a horrible dream and there was Alice with a cup of tea in her hand. A huge feeling of relief flooded through me. 'I had a horrible dream,' I told her. 'I was lost in the ruined and deserted streets of Grozny.' 'There are no ruins any more,' she said, lying down beside me. 'Everything is spotlessly new. Built to the latest specifications. They have covered hell over so that not even the tiniest chink shows through.' Then I really did wake up, with her voice in my head saying: 'Not even the tiniest chink. The tiniest chink. The tiniest chink.' I was trembling but at the same time I could still feel the warmth of her body all down my right-hand side.

— Horrible, the old lady says.

— It wasn't exactly horrible, Helena says. There was the warmth of her presence, not only the physical warmth of her body, but of her presence, bringing me that cup of tea. That was the most powerful feeling I took away from it.'

— Do you often dream about her? Ruth asks.

— I haven't for a long time, Helena says.

— I wonder if she dreams about you, Ruth says.

— What a funny thing to say.

— Why?

— I don't know. Why should she? I don't exist for her.

— You don't know that, Ruth says.

— I never have, Helena says, and since she went to Chechnya less than ever.

— You don't think she dreams about you sitting at your desk, lost in your work?

Helena laughs.

— Why not? Ruth says.

— I don't exist for her, Helena says. Full stop.

— Who's to say? Ruth says.

Helena is silent.

— What is it? Ruth says.

— I'm lost, Helena says.

— Lost?

— With my book.

— In a good or a bad way?

— Bad. Definitely. I've actually abandoned work on it. I just sit and talk to myself.

— Come round and talk to me instead.

— On paper, Helena says. I talk to myself on paper. I scribble whatever comes into my head hoping it will take me somewhere. But so far it hasn't and I can't see anything coming of it.

— That means it's going to be a real book, Ruth says.

— I wish I had your optimism, Helena says.

— I know what I'm talking about, Ruth says.

— It's not going to be a book at all, Helena says. I feel it slipping away from me day by day.

— Well, that's possible, Ruth says. But if it does turn out to be a book it will be a real one. Earned.

— Are you saying my other books were false?

— You're looking for a quarrel, Helena, Ruth says. You know very well I didn't say that. Besides, you had your doubts about them too. Only you've forgotten.

— Did I? Helena says.

— Of course you did, Ruth says. Only you've forgotten. You only remember the good bits.

Now she's going to say it's like childbirth, Helena thinks.

— It's a bit like childbirth, Ruth says.

— I think it's different with this one, Helena says.

— That's what you always say, Ruth says.

— No, I really think it's different. ·

— You always say that too, Ruth says.

# A Tall Stack of Danish

'Another new friend was Hedda Sterne, a Bucharest-born painter, who arrived in New York in 1941 and first met Cornell at the home of Peggy Guggenheim. Sterne, too, knew of Cornell's predilection for sweets. She would prepare "a tall stack of Danish" in anticipation of his visits and recalls him eating "ten or twelve Danish" in a single sitting. Despite this, she later said: "I always had the feeling that if I shook him he would pulverize into dust, like old paper".' (Solomon)

'The film-maker Stan Brakhage would often go round to the house in Flushing where Cornell would prepare a meal for them: "Three sardines, crackers and a glass of pink lemonade was a typical lunch," Brakhage said.' (ibid.)

'His usual practice was to wake around 6.30 and savor the morning's spirit of "freshness" before heading downtown around eleven o'clock. Arriving at Bickford's with a book under his arm, he would read while consuming some sort of junk food — his latest weakness was for French fries. There he would catch up on his diary, jotting down his thoughts and sightings of young girls — "teeners", as he called them.' (ibid.)

John Ashbery: 'We sat for a long time in the kitchen, which was devoid of any of the treasures we had imagined the house to be full of, drinking Lipton's tea and trying to do justice to the plate of leaden pastries on the table (Cornell explained that he preferred these "heavy-duty pastries" as he called them, the old-style cafeteria ones, to the newer, fancier ones).'

Mary Ann Caws, the editor of his journal and notebooks: 'He washed *his socks in the sink, used his tea bags five times, and held on to everything.'*

*MAC: 'Cornell's typical diet for a day in 1946 included caramel pudding, a few doughnuts, cocoa, white bread, peanut butter, peach jam, a Milky Way, some chocolate éclairs, a half-dozen sweet buns, a peach pie, a cake with icing, a prune twist. In the 1950s he was often seen picking at cottage cheese, toast, bologna, jello, and milk.'*

*'Lunch in a diner, banana creme pie, doughnut, and drink.' (Journal, 1 March 1947)*

*The art dealer, Alexander Jolas, remembered his astonishment at the food Joseph prepared for Robert: 'He loved his brother,' Jolas said, 'and the meals he made for him always consisted of the most incredible colours. . . He used to squeeze violets on top of mushroom soup to make it lilac-coloured.' (Solomon)*

*Carolee Schneemann, the performance artist: 'They had this intense close-ness, like they were the same being, only one had been stricken.'*

*'After the death of his brother his part-time help, Alexander Anderson, noted that he never seemed to eat: "I would prepare him dinner but he wouldn't touch it. He ate only this wretched cake, the kind from supermar-kets with thick white frosting."' (Solomon)*

*'After the death of his mother he liked to invite people to tea. His style of entertaining was far from lavish. Cornell might offer his guests a slice of cake and a cup of tea, while removing just a single tea-bag from the box. "Everyone would have the same tea-bag," said the designer Diane von Fürstenberg, who knew Cornell in his later years. "Then he'd pour us another cup of hot water and send the same tea-bag round again." If they were lucky he would take them on a tour of the house.' (Solomon)*

*(Scenario for a book: Cornell invites half a dozen of these beautiful and elegant young New York women to tea in his now empty house. He offers them a cup of tea using a single tea-bag and talks to them in his rambling and compulsive way about his life and his dreams. Mixture of memory and*

*fantasy. Monotonous voice, never letting up. In the midst of this he offers to take them on a tour of the house. We never hear them, only his rambling answers to their questions. Perhaps their voices first, a chorus: 'He had asked us for five o'clock. When we arrived he opened the door and stared at us as if he had never seen us before.' Etc.*

*The trouble with this is that it turns him into a 'a turn'. Don't want that. Don't want it at all.*

*Yet that is part of it.)*

## No Problem

— I was wondering when you were planning to leave, she
says.

— You want me to go?

— You can't stay here indefinitely, she says. The flat's much
too small. Besides, I want to be alone.

— No problem, he says.

— It is a problem, she says.

— No no. No problem.

— Have you found a job then?

— Maybe.

— Maybe you should go back to Czechoslovakia.

— Czech Republic.

— Maybe you should go back. Your family must be
expecting you.

— I will see my family, he says. But first I must be in London.

— So when do you think this job will materialise?

— Pardon me?

— When do you think you'll find a job?

— Maybe tomorrow.

— You can't go on living here forever, she says.

— Two three days more, he says.

— And if I asked you to go now?

— No problem, he says.

— What would you do?

— No problem. I tell you.

— You won't tell me what you'd do?

He shrugs.

— All right, she says. Stay for a day or two more and then that's it. OK?

— No problem, he says.

— You have to keep on repeating that?

— Pardon me?

— Never mind.

— You want me to go now, I go, he says. You are kind to have me all this time.

— That's all right, she says.

— I appreciate it, Helena.

— I'm glad you do.

— And tonight I take you out to eat.

— Take me out? With what?

— We go to a restaurant, he says. To celebrate.

— Celebrate what?

He laughs.

— That we meet, perhaps?

— And with what do you pay?

— I have money, he says.

— You have?

— Sure.

— How come?

— I have.

— Well, I'm glad to hear it, she says.

— So, tonight.

— I'm not sure, she says. I should stay in and work.

— You work all the time, Helena, he says. That is not the way to advance.

— No?

— Do you advance?

— No, she says, laughing.

— You see, he says. You sit at your desk and like that your conscience is clear. But you need to step aside and enjoy yourself and wait for something to happen.

— I tried that, she says. It doesn't work either.

— Perhaps you don't try hard enough.

— I tried as hard as I could.

— Maybe you don't want to write this book, he says.

— Maybe, she says. I've tried letting it go. Starting something else. But it keeps worming its way back into my mind.

— Maybe you need a lover, he says.

— Everybody tells me that, she says.

— Perhaps because it is true.

— You're ridiculous, she says.

— I do not say husband, he says. I say lover.

— I heard you.

— OK, he says. No problem.

— The problem is, she says, there is a problem.

— My mother always say: If there is a problem there is a solution.

— Your mother was a wise woman.

— Her mother say that too.

— What a family, she says.

— Yes, he says. Full of wisdom.

— Full of words, she says.

— But words is sometimes right, he says.

## From Another Lady

— Very nice, she says, as they wait for their coffee. On a hot evening like this you almost feel you're in Europe.

— You want to feel yourself in Europe? he asks.

— Yes, she says.

— But England can never be Europe.

— No, she says. Perhaps not. But what is it then?

— Look at the houses, he says. These small English houses with small rooms for small English people.

— But the English are big, she protests. Compared to the Czechs, for instance.

— But they live in small houses. With small rooms.

— I don't think they're that small, she says. But I know what you mean. None of the big apartment blocks which you see in every European city.

Their coffee arrives.

— Little rooms, he says. And then behind, little gardens.

— Lots of gardens, she says.

— But so little. So thin.

— But now you can get to Paris in two hours by train it's beginning to feel part of Europe. London is, at least.

— But without the traumas of Europe, he says. The traumas are what make Europe what it is today. Not the big apartments.

— You think so?

— The guilt. The shame. That is not found here.

— Guilt about other things perhaps? she says.

— Perhaps, he says. I do not know.

— Sexual things, she says.

— Maybe. I do not know.

He sips his coffee. He says:

— The shame of collaboration is still strong in Europe. First with the Nazis. And then with the Communists. Forced or free, it is always collaboration. People cannot forget these things.

— But they will in time, no?

— You think so?

— Don't you?

— No, he says. I do not think so. Always, there is new collaboration. New reasons for shame.

— It's still there?

— In Slovakia, he says. Hungary. Poland. Perhaps this fascism is the normal thing in our part of Europe, in China, in other places. And your democracy in England and America is the exception.

— And France and Germany and Scandinavia?

— You know, he says, for Putin and the leaders in Iran and China, Europe and America are old and tired and soon they will be bankrupt too. Maybe this Enlightenment that everybody thought would triumph over the world, with its human rights and rule of law and free markets and free spirits — perhaps that has lived its life, two hundred, two hundred and fifty years, and now it will die.

— You keep saying that, she says. It's a pretty frightening thought.

— Yes, he says. But that is how they think. Believe me.

— I want to walk, she says.

— I finish my coffee.

She waits.

— Now we go, he says.

He pays and they go up the street towards the Heath.

— My favourite view of London, she says after a while, pointing up to where the people and kites are visible on the hill top against the evening sun.

They walk.

— I love the slope of the hill and the sense of all that movement up there and people almost taking off into the sky, she says.

— They are swimming there, he says, pointing.

— Yes, that's the men's pond.

— You have to swim men and women separately? he asks.

— Don't look so horrified, she says. There's a mixed pond too, on the Hampstead side.

— Perhaps we swim one day? he asks.

— One day?

— Why not?

— I thought you were only here for another couple of days?

— Perhaps tomorrow?

They walk.

— Perhaps, she says.

— With my wife, he says, we often swim in the river. You lie on your back and the current will take you under many bridges. On the bridges, people waving. Then it is very difficult to swim back.

— Because of the current?

— Yes.

— It sounds wonderful, she says.

— Yes, he says.

— When was the last time you did this?

— Long time ago, he says.

— Why a long time ago?

— She is not my wife any more.

— Why not?

— Oh, he says. You want to know too much.

— I'm curious, she says.

— I go away for work, he says. And when I come back she does not want me any more.

— Just like that?

— Yes.

— She has someone else?

— Yes.

— And your son?

— My son, you see, he is from another lady.

— Another lady? Not your wife?

— No.

— Before or after your wife?

— Before.

— And she is married, this other lady?

— Yes. All married.

— All except you.

He laughs. — Yes, he says.

— Would you like to be married?

— One day.

— It doesn't really go with your job, marriage, does it?

— It is difficult. Perhaps if I meet the right lady.

They walk.

— And what would the right lady be like? she asks.

— Like you, he says.

— Me? She laughs. I wasn't asking you to be gallant, she says.

— Pardon me?

— Never mind.

They walk.

— Why like me? she asks.

— Why? He shrugs. Then he laughs.

He stops. He takes hold of her shoulders and turns her towards him. He looks into her eyes.

— Well? she says, holding his look.

He lets go, shrugs again.

They walk.

— We can cut across here, she says. We can get a bus on the Hampstead side.

They walk.

— When I came before I came from this direction, he says.

— When did you come?

— When I was a student. We saw everything. St Paul's. Tower of London. Houses of Parliament. Hampstead Heath.

They walk.

— And then you ended up in Grozny, she says.

He laughs. — No sightseeing in Grozny, he says.

— Perhaps now there's stability there, she says, they'll open the region up to tourism.

— You're a funny lady, he says.

— Bad taste, she says.

— They will try perhaps, he says. The mountains are very beautiful. Many waterfalls. The sound is amazing.

– Perhaps when they start having weekend breaks to Grozny I'll go and see Alice, she says.

– Pardon me?

– You know, three nights for £450 for three-star hotel, breakfast included.

He shakes his head.

– Not many hotels in Grozny? she says.

– No.

– The Kadyrov Palace Hotel?

– Not yet.

– Not very funny, she says. Sorry.

– No problem, he says.

The bus arrives.

# Houdini

*It was at the Hippodrome on Sixth Avenue at Forty-Third Street that the young Joseph Cornell first saw Harry Houdini perform.*

*Born Erik Weisz in Budapest in 1874, one of the seven sons of Rabbi Samuel Weisz, Houdini had come to the States in 1878, and was by the first decade of the twentieth century the most famous escape artist of his day. It seemed there was no situation so desperate he could not find a way out. Handcuffed and locked in a metal box dropped to the bottom of a deep pit, he would still manage to get out.*

*Cornell would never forget his first sight of the great man. In one of his letters home from school he wrote to his mother: 'I was ready to give a speech on Houdini, but was not called on.'*

*That sentence sums him up: 'I was ready to give a speech on Houdini, but was not called on.' Just the facts, no clue as to how he felt. But it says more than whole paragraphs of analysis. For him, he senses, there was no escape, precisely because no-one had locked him in, or out. The world seemed simply unaware of him or his needs.*

*Since he was not called on it is probable that his schoolmates never discovered his passion for, his identification with, Houdini. But for those who contemplate the boxes he made in the course of his life, it is clear that Houdini was not forgotten. 'The metal rings and suspended chains that would later become elements in his boxes,' Deborah Solomon suggests, 'refer at least partly to Houdini and the memory of the lonely boy who wished to vanish from the shackles of earthly reality.'*

*That reality — of his own body, of his absurd and overbearing mother, of his beloved brother doomed never to be able to walk or speak properly — became ever more oppressive when his father, the Houdini-like travelling salesman who had the habit of reappearing suddenly in the family home after long absences, entertaining the children with entrancing tales of adventure in faraway places, and then disappearing again as suddenly as he had come, died when Cornell was fourteen. He must have sensed then that the chains had been well and truly fastened round him. His sister told Lindsay Blair in 1980: 'Before Daddy died — that was when he had a full sense of security. As soon as Daddy died he felt that he should be the man of the house. And that's when all his dreams and terrible nightmares started. You know, in Andover he had a terrible time. He used to have these terrible nightmares and he'd yell for me. I would find myself running up the stairs, not even awake, saying "I'm coming, I'm coming". At one time he was cowering in a corner and he said "It's a white antelope, it's a white antelope", and I didn't turn the light on, you know, I had learnt not to startle him. So I said: "It's alright Joe, it's just a sheet." It was hard to convince him because he was in the grip of terror.'*

*His fantasy life became full of escape artists of different kinds: nineteenth-century ballerinas like Fanny Cerrito and Marie Taglioni, who, in the accounts left by their contemporaries, hardly seemed to inhabit the earth at all, soaring heavenwards en pointe, miraculously released from the laws of gravity; film stars like Hedy Lamarr and Lauren Bacall, whose lives, flickering on the white screen in the dark of the cinema, or splashed across the pages of the fanzines Cornell collected, seemed to unfold in the most luxurious hotels and with the most glamorous of men, though that did not seem to free them from the aura of sorrow and doom that shrouded them; and the little girls he filmed in parks and by fountains, surrounded by pigeons, their pigtails and white dresses flying in the wind, at one with the birds. What he felt with all of them was that they did not belong to our cruel and capricious* world. Miraculously, they seemed to rise above it. And we were drawn to them because they gave us a taste of what it was like to be on the other side. Yet, if we tried to grasp them, pin them down, they either died in our hands or ran away. So the question became: How to hold on to them and yet allow them their freedom? That is why, the polar opposite of Hitchcock in this, he did not want control in his films, either of the female protagonists or of the direction in which the film itself should go. To Stan Brakhage, the film-maker who worked with him, giving him technical advice and usually holding the camera, he said simply: 'Start the camera, see what happens for a while, then stop it.' The results were magical: not Hitchcock but not Warhol either. Each short film like a Debussy prelude, tiny and miraculous in its combination of freedom and a deep underlying sense of rhythm and form. Pure Cornell.

His first boxes he called 'soap-bubble sets', and he usually included a real old clay pipe lying on a shelf at the front, while behind, glued to the back, an image of the heavens or the earth cut out from a magazine or from one of his many books on popular astronomy — our universe, but also a mere bubble, blown by a child from a pipe, here for a second and gone the next. The soap bubble was a perfect image for what he was after: a momentary reflection and symbol of our world, which bursts as it soars upwards. Cornell has not been given enough credit for the sureness of his choice of these initial conceits — soap bubble, birdcage, heavenly hotel — which give to his best boxes their resonance and authority.

The nearest he came to flying himself was on his bicycle in the garden centre years. 'Walking produces fatigue,' he wrote in his diary, 'car takes too much for granted, but on your bicycle you are both flying and part of the world.'

Lauren Bacall. He first sees her in a movie-theatre in Flushing on a rainy Monday afternoon, and at once notes her 'Javanese' face. In the box-homage he constructs for her the wandering ball, in Deborah Solomon's interpretation, 'suggests a man who is in and out of Bacall's life and has a special familiarity with the details concerning her'.

To this one wants to reply: Surely the 'wandering ball' is just that, a ball that is free to move down the conduits and through the holes he has constructed for it. But that would be as wrong as Solomon's too firm allegory. It's more than 'just a ball', just as it's less than 'a man who is in and out of Bacall's life'. But what is it then? The beauty of the box, like so many others, is that it tells no story, preaches no sermon, yet, like music, it resonates within us, setting free a whole range of possibilities.

It's a complex game he plays with the viewer of this and of the other great boxes he constructed in the fifties, the Medici Slot Machine and Gilles, his homage to Watteau and the Commedia dell'arte. At their centre are images of otherworldly figures, dreamers, set in the penny-arcade world of the urban America of the thirties and forties, and they all three assert the paradoxical truth that it is only possible for art to assert: Go ahead, they seem to say, dream with the dreamer, but never forget that the dreamer will wake up in a world devoid of dreams.

There was, as it happens, a rival to Houdini in the imagination of Joseph Cornell, a native-born escape artist, even more famous in her time than Houdini: Mary Baker Eddy, the founder of Christian Science. 'In dreams we fly to Europe and meet a far-off friend,' she wrote. 'The looker-on sees the body in the bed, but the supposed inhabitant of that body carries it through the air and across the ocean. This shows the power of thought.'

The power of thought — that is Mary Baker Eddy's message and it can of course accomplish far more than Houdini or nineteenth-century ballerinas could ever offer. Cornell was naturally receptive to her message. He was twenty-three when he joined a Christian Science church and he remained a firm believer all his life. He studied Mrs Baker Eddy's writings, he regularly attended services, he subscribed to the Christian Science Monitor, and he not only spent a great deal of time in the Christian Science reading-room in Flushing, but was an active helper there. As with his other activities, this part of his life was kept strictly apart from the rest: few of his fellow employees when he was a cloth salesman, or, later, of his artist friends, knew of his Christian Science affiliations, and none of his fellow Christian Scientists knew of his growing artistic reputation. His mother hated it, but then his mother's disapproval had never deterred him. He and Robert became committed followers.

Mary Baker Eddy is both forthright and charmingly modest in her magnum opus, the effective Bible of Christian Science, Science and Health, with Key to the Scriptures. 'The adoption of scientific religion and of divine healing,' she writes, 'will ameliorate sickness and death.' Quite what it means to 'ameliorate' death, she does not say. Throughout she is splendidly brisk and firm: 'The ancient Christians were healers. Why has this element of Christianity been lost?' she asks. 'Man's control of the universe, including man, is no longer an open question,' she insists, 'but is demonstrable Science.' The demonstration seems to consist in her presenting her readers with examples of her healing powers and with testimonies from grateful erstwhile sufferers from such diverse ailments as chronic constipation, rheumatoid arthritis, sprained ankles and much much more. All, they inform us, were healed by Christian Science, and all are eternally grateful to its founder.

At its heart her message is simple: 'Admit the existence of matter and you admit that mortality (and therefore disease) has a foundation in fact. Deny the existence of matter and you can destroy the belief in material conditions.'

One can see the attraction of such a message for Cornell, and even more for Robert. No need here of Houdini-like exertions, only that mysterious thing, belief in the words of Mrs Baker Eddy.

It is because Cornell was a Christian Scientist that he went on writing to his mother and to Robert after their deaths, went on buying presents for *them and for poor murdered Joyce Hunter, when they were no longer there to receive them. For Cornell they had merely escaped the prison of the body. Soon he would be joining them.*

*Did he really believe that death was a mere epiphenomenon, the product of our material and blinkered vision? With a part of himself, no doubt he did. But that did not assuage his grief. Everyone who saw him in those last years, when he was living alone in the house on Utopia Parkway, commented on the fact that he seemed to be a man in deep depression. Cornell, however, kept his counsel.*

## Now

— Languorous, she says.

— Pardon me?

— What I feel, she says.

She lies back on the platform, her feet in the water, and looks up at the sky.

Time passes.

She closes her eyes.

There is a splash. She sits up, looks at the damp patch beside her, and searches for his head among the swimmers.

She sits up and watches as he slowly swims back to the platform through the mass of bodies.

He climbs out of the water and sits beside her.

— Nice? she asks.

— Very nice.

— You think I should go in?

— Yes.

She slides off the platform into the icy water.

Gradually, as she swims out, towards the clearer water, where there are fewer people, her body starts to warm up.

She lies on her back and looks up at the sky and at the trees that surround the pond.

When she returns he is lying on the platform on his towel. She lies down beside him.

The cloudless sky again.

He leans on his elbow, looking down at her.

– What is it? she asks.

He bends over and kisses her on the mouth. She pushes him away.

They lie.

– That was good, she says.

– The kiss or the swim?

She is silent.

– I think so too, he says.

Time passes.

– I'm starting to feel cold, she says.

– You want to go?

– Soon.

– I swim one more time, he says, and dives in.

She goes inside to change.

When she emerges he is already dressed and waiting for her.

– Shall we go? she says.

– Yes.

– No problem?

He laughs.

– No problem, he says.

In the flat she says: – I want to go to bed with you. Now.

– Me too, he says.

Afterwards she says:

– That doesn't mean I will want to go to bed with you again. You understand?

He is silent.

– You understand? she asks again.

— No problem, he says.

— I'm glad, she says. I don't want problems.

— No problem, he says.

# Body in Boot

— That's what it says, Ruth says, holding the paper out to her. Body in boot.

Helena takes it from her.

She reads out loud: — 'Mr Simon Pretzel, father of four, of St John's Close, Islington, told the police: "When I opened the boot of the car, there he was, with a wad of cloth in his mouth and his wrists and ankles tied with cord."'

— Can you imagine? Ruth says. Opening the boot of your car and finding a body inside.

Helena is scanning the paper. — A Chinaman, it says here, she says. What's that about?

— It must be gang-related, Ruth says, pouring herself a cup of tea. London's full of Chinese mafia.

— A total stranger, he says, Helena says. But they've taken him in for questioning.

Ruth is staring down at her cup.

— They don't think he did it, do they? Helena says. Why would he put the body in his own boot and then go to the police?

— You never know why people do things, Ruth says. You can do all sorts of unlikely things on the spur of the moment.

— You don't tie someone's wrists and ankles with cord on the spur of the moment, Helena says.

— You lose your head, Ruth says. You do irrational things.

— It must have been an awfully big car, Helena says.

— Chinamen are pretty small, Ruth says. You'd be hard put to it to bundle a Swede into the boot of a car.

— You think that's why they chose a Chinaman? Helena says. Because of his size?

— You're talking nonsense, dear, Ruth says.

— I mean why they thought of the boot of a car.

— I'm sure it was all pre-planned, Ruth says. These gangland executions are always carried out with precision.

— I didn't know you knew so much about it, Helena says.

— I watch films like everybody else, Ruth says.

Helena stands up. — I've got to go, she says. Will you be all right?

— Why on earth not? Ruth says. I haven't been stuffed into the boot of a car, have I?

— No, Helena says. But it's happened awfully close to here.

— I doubt if it's the work of a serial killer, Ruth says.

— Anyway, give me a ring if you want company, Helena says.

— You know I'll always do that, dear, Ruth says.

## Soon Enough

— Now you've got your friend staying, Tom says, you've got no time for me at all.

— Are you jealous of him?

— Profoundly.

— Why?

— Because you never have time for me now.

— I do have my work to do, Helena says.

— You used to manage to combine the two, Tom says.

— Don't complain, she says. Here I am.

— And how's it going?

— What?

— Your work.

— So-so.

— Meaning?

— Meaning so-so.

— And?

— And what?

He is silent.

— I'm exploring, she says. Trying out things. We'll see.

— Why so secretive? he asks.

— I'm not being secretive.

— What do you call it then?

— I'm just in the middle and don't really want to talk about it.

— But I'm interested in your work, Tom says.

— Thank you, she says.

— Don't thank me. It's interesting work.

She is silent.

— The last time you were here you told me you were thinking of jettisoning chronology.

— I don't want to talk about it.

— But I need to know. For my own book. About the two sisters.

— Oh stop it, she says.

— Tell me about Ed, he says.

— What about him?

— Has he found a job? When's he leaving? Is he going back to Chechnya? That sort of thing.

— He thinks he's found a job. He doesn't know when he's leaving. He's not going back to Chechnya. At least for the moment.

— What's that mean?

— They'd like him to but it's too dangerous. He couldn't get in as a bona fide journalist. He'd have to sneak in. It's not worth it.

— Bona fide journalist, he says. Well well.

— He might go to one of the neighbouring republics. Apparently that's where the next big story will break.

— Why?

— Because you can't really stamp out rebellion. You crush it in one place and it springs up in another. The Christian Church knew that very well in its early years. The only way to win is to enlist those you would convert to your own side. Don't destroy their temples, turn them into churches. Don't destroy their stories, give them your meaning. Spoil the Egyptians.

— Spoil the what?

— It's a phrase of St Augustine's. A reference to the Exodus. The Hebrews got out, but they took the jewels of the Egyptians with them.

— But spoil?

— Despoil. Take their things as spoil.

— Oh, Tom says. I see.

— But the Russians aren't like that, she says. They think you need to show force and the subject peoples will cower. It's a mistake all colonial powers make, and it never works. It didn't work in South Africa. It didn't work in Afghanistan. And it isn't working in the Caucasus. All they've succeeded in doing by setting up this puppet regime is to fan the flames of Islamic resentment. So now Ingushetia is flaring up, and after that it will be another and another and another. Afghanistan will be a picnic compared with this.

— Afghanistan didn't belong to the Soviets. These places legally belong to Russia.

— That's not the way the Chechens see it.

— It's the way the Russians see it.

— I don't know enough about it, she says. But that's where he says they're thinking of sending him.

— Soon, I hope, Tom says.

— Soon enough, she says.

— Doesn't it strike you as odd that this chap should have been allowed to stay in Chechnya for years and years?

— I don't think it was years and years, she says.

— A hell of a long time, he says. Long after the other journalists had left.

— What are you implying?

— I don't know. I just find it odd. Was anyone employing him? And if so what kind of pictures was he sending back?

— What are you suggesting?

— I don't know. I just find it odd.

— Perhaps he was compiling a travel brochure for the Kadyrov government, she says.

— That's what I was wondering, he says.

## That Was Then

— That was then, Helena says.

— Then? he says.

— Oh, lighten up, she says,

— I do not understand.

— I don't want to explain.

— Because you thought I was leaving you sleep with me? he asks.

— Lighten up, she says. I've got work to do.

— Helena, he says, we must go on a long trip together.

— Sure, she says.

— Today, he says.

— Sure, she says. But I have work to do first.

— When do you finish your work?

— Ed, she says. You told me you'd be out of here by Monday. It's Thursday today and you're still here.

— I will stay till you say you will come with me.

— I'm not going anywhere, she says.

— Helena, he says, you cannot do this to me.

— Watch me, she says.

— I will stay here, he says.

— No you won't, she says. I will throw your stuff onto the pavement and change the locks.

He laughs.

— See if I don't, she says.

She gets up.

— Where are you going? he asks.

— It's none of your business, she says.

— Helena, he says.

— Go back to Alice, she says.

— Alice? he says. What is Alice doing in this?

She goes to the door. — I told you, she says. If you are not gone by this evening I will change the locks.

— Why do you do this to me? he says.

— Because that's how I am, she says.

# I Saw Fanny Cerrito

*By the time he was in his late sixties Cornell had in fact outlived the Surrealists, who hit America in the thirties, the neo-Romantics, who were all the rage in the forties, the Abstract Expressionists, who ruled the roost throughout the fifties, and even many of the Pop Artists who came into prominence in the sixties. He was almost an institution. And though never as well known to the general public as Dalí and Tchelitchew, Pollock and Warhol, he was an object of fascination to many. No Saul Bellow though. He was fascinating not because of his looks or his aura but because he seemed to those who met him to have already crossed over to some other world. When you see photos of him in his old age, alone in that house on Utopia Parkway, after the death of his brother and his mother, his skin seems papery, his eyes gaze into another world. He still slept in the narrow bed that had always been his, in a room full of his files and boxes crammed with cuttings. Not that he slept much. He seems to have spent most nights sitting in the kitchen, the oven on and the oven door open, reading or just staring into space. But these gorgeous emancipated young women kept making the journey out to Flushing to see him. 'I would sit down beside him on the narrow bed,' Leila Hadley told Deborah Solomon, 'and he would lie very still beside me. Sometimes I undressed him and sucked him off. I felt he liked that. I felt it calmed him.' 'My heart went out to him,' she says elsewhere, 'but he seemed very far away. Already on the other side.'*

*But was he not always on the other side?*

*True, but you feel that at the end, with Robert no longer there to do things* for and with his mother no longer there to fight against and prove himself to, he no longer had any reason to live. Even Mary Baker Eddy wasn't much help any more. She had been his ally in the fight to keep control of his life. To keep him from falling into despair at the way fate had treated him. But in the end she had abandoned him, like the others. Or perhaps not. Perhaps I've got it all wrong and he just waited for death, certain that at that moment the veil would be lifted and he would be at peace at last in a better and a fairer world.

Or perhaps he didn't know himself which of the two views he held. Or he held one of them one moment and the other the next. Or both at once.

In the first interview he ever gave, in 1957, he said: 'Two things changed my life: the first was a visit to a pet shop in Morpeth, Long Island, when I heard a voice and saw a light. And the second was on West Fifty-Second Street. I saw Fanny Cerrito on top of the Manhattan Storage Warehouse.'

So perhaps he really did live the Romantic dream. The dream of Novalis and Nerval. And we do him a disservice by feeling pity for him. It is he who should be pitying us, who have never seen our equivalent of Fanny Cerrito on top of the Manhattan Storage Warehouse.

Do I believe that?

I don't know. I think of how everyone commented on how depressed he seemed at the end. As though he had nothing to live for. And if he had good friends like Leila Hadley who could make things a little easier while he waited to join Fanny and Joyce and Robert, who would begrudge him that?

Yet when I think about his last years I find I have tears in my eyes. But perhaps that only says something about me and the state I'm in rather than anything about him.

That is not the last word.

(But what is?)

## I Know You Are There

— When are you going to get a decent bed? she asks.

— This one suits me fine, Tom says.

— It may suit you but it's not very comfortable for two, she says.

— How often do you sleep with me? he asks.

— I won't sleep with you again unless you buy a bigger bed, she says.

— And if I do will you sleep with me every night?

— You wouldn't want to sleep with me every night, she says.

— And if I did?

— No, she says.

— No what?

— No I wouldn't sleep with you every night if you bought a bigger bed.

— Then what's the point?

— Because if you don't I won't sleep with you at all.

— You always say that, he says, and then you always do.

— This time I'm serious, she says.

— I know you're serious, he says. But then you forget.

— I won't forget, she says. This is practically a single bed.

— It is what is known in the trade as a small double.

— That's what I mean, she says. Practically a single.

— I'd feel awful sleeping by myself night after night in a big double, he says.

— But I feel awful sleeping with you in this.

— I like having you here, he says.

There is the sudden sound of someone climbing the steps to the front door.

The bell rings in the flat above them.

They wait.

It rings again.

They wait.

A man's voice says, in a loud whisper: — Helena!

They hold their breaths.

— Helena, he says again. Are you there, Helena? It's me. Ed.

He must be leaning over the wall because he now taps on the side window directly above them.

— Helena, he says. You have to open. I do not have anywhere to go.

They wait.

— Helena, he says. I know you are there.

They wait.

A silence.

They hear him descend the stairs.

He stops. He opens the iron gate leading down to the basement flat.

They wait.

They hear him moving off down the street.

After a while she says:

— I'm sorry.

— You think it's true?

— What?

— That he doesn't have anywhere to go?

— How should I know? she says.

— You don't think you were a bit hard on him?

— That's right, she says. Take his side.

She lies rigid in the dark beside him.

— Relax, he says. He won't come back.

She is silent, eyes open, staring into the dark.

— Lena, he says. Please.

He feels her body tense beside him in the narrow bed.

— Lena, he says again. Please.

## Custos Messium

She says to the old lady:

— I'm excited. I think I've got my conclusion, if nothing else.

— Tell me, Ruth says.

— At the very end of his life, she says, opening her note-book out on the table in front of her, on 14 November 1972, six weeks before his death, he wrote in his diary:

'3 stars over the maple that

used to stand sentinel companion

to the whole white birch

NW

Beaut. soft nebulous

Dark grey raining

Slightly

PEACE at midnight

And for the night!'

So, she says, we have to understand how profoundly he felt that the stars were companions and protectors of both him and his house. The last collage he ever made, dated 2 March 1971, consists of a photograph of his beloved quince tree in his back yard, across which he has inscribed two enormous dark brown shadows. On the back he has pasted a photostat of Flammarion's chart of the 'Neighbours of the Pole', those constellations which cluster round the North Pole:

Cameleopardis, the giraffe, and Custos Messium, the custodian of the harvest. Then, along with his signature, he has
pasted the words: 'RESIDENTS 05841/37-08 UTOPIA
PARKWAY/FLUSHING NY 11350.'

— Custos Messium, she says. The custodian of the harvest
in Latin. Does it mean anything to you?

— I'm afraid not, the old lady says. I never managed to get
to grips with the stars, though I'd like to have done. I mean I
like to look up at the sky if I'm out at night but I can never
see the beasts people claim to see up there.

— Me too, Helena says. But working on Cornell has forced
me to think about all that. It seems that Custos Messium is a
constellation discovered and named by the astronomer Jérome
Lalande in 1775 in honour of his friend Charles Messier, the
'keeper of the constellations', as he was known. It is located
between the camel-leopard, Cassiopeia and Cepheus.
Cameleopardis is often called The Giraffe because that is what
he looks like, and Cassiopeia was the boastful wife of King
Cepheus and the mother of Andromeda.

— You told me about the Cassio thing and Andromeda, the
old lady says, but I can't remember what you said.

— That must have been when I told you about what I
consider to be Cornell's greatest work, the box known as *Hotel
Andromeda*, Helena says. But it isn't important here, except to
show how constant his interest in the stars was, since that box
dates from almost twenty years earlier.

— I remember now, Ruth says. She was chained to a rock.

— Exactly, Helena says. Anyway, one of the interesting
things about Custos Messium is that the constellation is no
longer recognised.

— What does that mean?

— Astronomers no longer regard it as a viable constellation.

— What's a viable constellation?

— Don't worry, Helena says. It's not important.

— But you said it was.

— You'll see, Helena says. Give me a chance.

— All right, the old lady says. Go on.

— The guardian of the harvest, Helena says. Perhaps because since Phoenician times that part of the skies over the North Pole has been associated with wheat fields. Whatever the reason, it was bound to strike a chord in Joseph Cornell. You remember the early collage I told you about, where he pictures Boötes with his foot stuck in a box which is meticulously drawn in classical perspective, as is a breadbox placed to the right of the collage and a sheaf of wheat next to it? Anyway, in September 1962 Cornell jots down a note after seeing a young boy going through a subway turnstile with his sister and mother. It's a note that takes us to the heart of his life and work I think: 'The gangling [*sic*] in khaki shorts and blue shirt, pushing through the stiles,' he writes, '... look of unspoilt youth, a kind of wandering, then, suddenly, in a flash... this "youth in blue" CUSTOS MESSIUM — the custodian — the wandering night companion of the "Little Bear" and Camel-leopard. He is a forgotten' — that is the point of my telling you the constellation is no longer recognised — 'he is a forgotten constellation, "cannot be seen with the naked eye" but for those "with eyes to see"...'

— For those with eyes to see, she says, — readers of Novalis or Nerval — or even followers of Mary Baker Eddy — what? An image of a beautiful youth, custodian of the harvest — but what harvest? – in the skies above, and at the same time entering the gates of the underground. The vision clearly aroused Cornell. The diary entry makes that clear. But why? How? The 'gangling', as yet unformed body, usually in Cornell belonging to young girls rather than young boys, is clearly an object of desire. But what does that mean? Does it mean we've hit rock bottom at last and found that desire for unformed girls and boys, only half repressed, drives his life and art? Think of all those androgynous figures from the Medici prince to the Grand Meaulnes, the idolised boy of Alain-Fournier's dream-novel, which meant so much to Cornell, of Lauren Bacall with her 'Javanese' face – they are everywhere in Cornell. But though our culture pushes us in this direction, we must resist. For Cornell's sake, but even more for our own. Why, after all, should physical desire trump everything else? There are many forms of desire and it may be that the physical is only an instance of something larger, more inclusive.

– To see the vision of the boy entering the subway merely as a figure of physical desire, she says, is to betray it. It is the conflation of a boy at the gates of the underground and the guardian of the harvest at the gates of heaven that makes Cornell's heart leap, not simply the vision of the boy. And what is this vision a vision of? Is it not at least partly a vision of Cornell's own youthful self before he entered the gates of life, before the disappearance of his father and the realisation that, though supremely unfit for the task, he would henceforth have to be the mainstay of his dysfunctional family? Is that not perhaps the real driver of paedophilia, a love of what one was before one became what one is, and a desire to return to that lost self by merging with it?

— The image, she goes on, is filled not only with desire but also with wonder. And it is strangely comforting. The boy, is, after all, a Guardian, Custos. He is the guardian of those lower depths where the grain is stored, as Cornell stored the leaves and branches he salvaged from beach and field in his cellar in the wonder years of the garden centre bicycle rides, and stored again in the boxes into which he incorporated them. For was he too not, in his way, a custodian of the harvest, the harvest he has now bequeathed to us? There he stands, as artists have always done, at the door, protecting his harvest and at the same time allowing us to partake of it without destroying ourselves in the process.

— In looking out at the night sky in those last lonely years as he sits in his back yard, she says, he looks out at an image of himself above and beyond time and space, which are all we usually know. An image both of himself and of that which is wholly other, for only that which is not oneself, which has been there before us and will still be there after us, can truly protect us. Yet it is also an image of something which has been forgotten, removed from the Book that incorporates all our current knowledge. His art will be a better book, more comprehensive, reminding us of what we have lost.

— I want my own book, she says, to bring him back into our consciousness in all his oddity and confusion, in all his pain and suffering, in all his cussedness and with all his maddening foibles, but also in his quality as a visionary, an ambiguous visionary, the only kind tolerable in our modern world.

She stops. She looks up at the old lady. — That's it, she says.

Slowly the old lady claps her hands.

— Does that make sense? Helena asks.

— I'll have to think about it, the old lady says. But you certainly carried me along as you were speaking.

— It's only the end, Helena says. I've got all the rest to do.

— When you've got the end you've got the whole thing, the old lady says. And you've got the passion to wrap it all up.

— Unless what I say is true, Helena says, passion is an entirely negative quality.

— I'm not so sure about that, the old lady says.


THE END

# Note

While writing this novel I have had a number of books constantly to hand:

*Joseph Cornell: Theater of the Mind. Selected Diaries, Letters and Files.* Edited by Mary Ann Caws. Thames and Hudson, 1973.

Mary Baker Eddy: *Science and Health, with Key to the Scriptures.* The Christian Science Board of Directors, 1903.

Kirsten Hoving: *Joseph Cornell and Astronomy.* Princeton University Press, 2009.

Kynaston McShine (ed.): *Joseph Cornell.* The Museum of Modern Art, New York, 1980.

Anna Politikovskaya: *A Dirty War: A Russian Reporter in Chechnya.* The Harvill Press, 2001.

Anna Politikovskaya: *A Small Corner of Hell: Despatches from Chechnya.* University of Chicago Press, 2003.

Deborah Solomon: *Utopia Parkway: The Life and Work of Joseph Cornell.* Pimlico, 1998.

Leo Tolstoy: *Hadji Murat,* in *Master and Man and Other Stories,* tr. Paul Foote. Penguin Books, 1977.

I have also been much helped by the following:

Lindsay Blair: *Joseph Cornell's Vision of Spiritual Order.* Reaktion

Books, 1998.

Robert Seely: *Russo-Chechen Conflict, 1800–2000: A Deadly Embrace*. Frank Cass, 2001.

Charles Simic: *Dime-Store Alchemy: The Art of Joseph Cornell*. The New York Review of Books, 1992.

Tony Wood: *Chechnya: The Case for Independence*. Verso, 2007.